Praise for Lena Matthew's *Call Me*

Rating 4 ½ lips

"Call Me was a fun, very well-written book that I devoured in one sitting. The transition that Kayla and Dylan take from being friends to lovers is *HOT*. Absolutely scorching....In addition to being wet-your-panties-sexy, Call Me is also laugh-out-loud funny."

~ *Kerin, Two Lips Reviews*

Blue Ribbon Rating: 4.5 blue ribbons

"CALL ME is the first book in Lena Matthews JOKERS WILD series and it starts it off with a resounding bang!... Let's face it the sex scenes are just too hot not to pick up a copy and read it for yourself....Wonderfully done Ms. Matthews!"

~ *Crissy Dionne, Romance Junkies*

Call Me
JOKER'S WILD

Lena Matthews

A SAMHAIN PUBLISHING, LTD. publication.

Samhain Publishing, Ltd.
512 Forest Lake Drive
Warner Robins, GA 31093
www.samhainpublishing.com

Editing by Jessica Bimberg
Cover by Scott Carpenter

First Samhain Publishing, Ltd. electronic publication: October 2006
First Samhain Publishing, Ltd. print publication: April 2007

Dedication

This book is dedicated to three wonderful people. To Duane, Kimberly and my lovely husband Leo. Thank you all for being understanding, supportive and, most all, for knowing how to take a joke. You guys made writing this book fun.

Chapter One

"Men suck."

Yawning, Dylan Thompson blinked several times to clear his sleep-clouded head as he held the phone closer to his ear. Male bashing wasn't the exact way he preferred to be woken up by a beautiful woman, but when the woman in question was one Kayla Martin, bum magnet extraordinaire, Dylan was all right with it. "Hello to you too, Kayla."

"I just had the date from hell," grumbled Kayla, his upstairs neighbor and best female bud. Then, as if she finally realized what time it was, she asked, "Were you sleeping?"

Turning over, he groaned at the tale-tell pain in his neck as he glanced at the clock on the VCR. It was only ten and he was already asleep. God, he was getting old. Far too old to be sleeping on the couch, that was for sure, especially when he had an extremely comfortable bed just a few feet away in his bedroom.

Dylan sat up on the couch and looked at the papers laid out around him. He was supposed to be working, but he had known Kayla was going out on a date and he wanted to be up to talk to her when she came home. Nothing was as amusing as a recap of her dates. "No, I was just finishing some last-minute work."

"With your eyes closed."

Dylan chuckled. She knew him so well. Almost as well as he knew her after five years of friendship, a friendship begun mainly out of boredom. They were the only single people under the age of fifty living in the building. Weeks of nodding in the hall and passing on the stairs led to quick hellos and small talk around the mailboxes, and before long Kayla and he were exchanging witty repartees at building meetings. Then one day, out of the blue, Kayla asked him over to look at her sink.

Accustomed to women hitting on him, Dylan was very surprised to find out there actually was something wrong with her sink. Although Kayla was a computer wiz, she had absolutely no mechanical skills.

It took him two years before he could convince her that her garbage disposal wasn't also moonlighting as a trash compactor. Just thinking of her little peccadilloes made him smile. Dylan wouldn't miss talking to her for all the sleep in the world.

"I was just resting my eyes."

"Sure you were," she laughed. "I'll let you get back to it then."

"No, I want to talk to you."

"I don't know. I feel awful."

"Why?"

"Because I woke you up just to bitch at you."

"That's what friends are for and besides, if I don't get my nightly dose of Kayla's capers, my day would just be incomplete." Dylan leaned back on the couch and ran his hand down his bare chest. "So what happened, Kay?"

"I'm going to die a virgin."

Dylan couldn't hold back his snort of laughter. "Highly unlikely, since you lost your virginity when you were seventeen."

"Well it's grown back or something. I read that it can happen. Born-again virgins or something like that."

Dylan shook his head and smiled. Kayla was notorious for getting facts wrong, which was highly amusing considering her genius-level IQ. "Did you read the entire article or just the headline?"

"Umm, I don't remember," Kayla paused as if in thought, "but that's beside the point. This guy was a complete loser."

"Kayla," Dylan interrupted. "You met him outside of court, what did you expect?"

"Lots of respectable men are at the courthouse."

The brat had the nerve to sound offended. "Yes, those are lawyers and judges, not people holding up their hands saying 'no pictures, no comments'."

"Shut up, he was not." She laughed.

He might as well have been though, because whether she wanted to admit it or not, Kayla had horrible taste in men. If there were a homeless, jobless guy in a radius of fifty miles, Kayla would find him, fall in love with him and take him home. Kayla liked men who were projects. Someone she could work with, nurture or help in any way. And that was the bane of her existence.

"That was low," she said, once she got herself back together.

Kayla's snickering made him smile broader. Dylan loved the way her voice resonated with joy when she laughed. It was a dry, hoarse sound that you could tell came from her soul. It was just one of the many things he liked about her; her voice, her laughter and her ability to make him hard with just a sentence.

"In the five years I've known you, have you ever had a good date?"

"Well...umm..."

Dylan could practically smell the smoke burning as she pondered her answer. "Yes, October nineteenth, my date took me to Disneyland."

"That was me, Kayla." Dylan dryly reminded her. Kayla's memory was as poor as her choice in clothes and men.

"Yeah, it was great."

"It wasn't a date."

"Sure it was. You paid and we had sex."

Shocked, Dylan didn't remember it that way, and unlike Kayla, his memory wasn't faulty. "We did not."

"I had sex with someone. Oh wait, never mind, I remember now, I masturbated. Sheesh, I'm depressed.

The last time I can remember having sex was with myself."

It was late, it was dark, and Kayla was talking about sex. Dylan couldn't think of a better way to spend the night.

"Do you want me to come up?" Leaning over, he turned on the lamp and blinked several times, trying to get his eyes to adjust to the light.

Kayla sighed. "No, you have to get up early in the morning."

"Well, I'm up now," he said as he stood. Stretching his long frame, Dylan ran his free hand through his short brown hair, mangling it more than the nap did. Looking down, he noticed his normal reaction to Kayla and sex in the same sentence, an erection. "In more ways than one I might add. I think it's because you said masturbation. So what—"

"Now, Dylan, why do all of our late night—"

"Or early morning," he interrupted. Kayla was a big fan of calling him, no matter what time it was.

"Pardon me," she chuckled. "Or early morning conversations have to end in..."

"So what are you wearing?" they both said at the same time. Smiling, Dylan walked into the dark hallway and entered his kitchen. Without turning on the light, he opened the refrigerator and rummaged through it, looking for a snack.

"And the answer is?" He bent down, opened the fruit drawer, and grabbed an apple. Taking a huge bite, he

11

shut the door and headed back towards his living room.

"Why?"

"You know why. I love your voice." One of the many things, he thought, sitting back down on the couch.

"You're very strange," she laughed. "Only you would think that my hoarse voice is sexy."

"I'm not strange."

"I sound like I need a throat lozenge," Kayla replied, laughing again.

"Oh no, it's very sexy." Just like the owner. Setting the apple on the table, Dylan gave another huge stretch and let out a moan of despair when he realized just how awake he was.

"I'm going to be up for hours now, thanks."

Kayla's voice was muffled and seemed as if she were in a tunnel.

"What are you doing?" Dylan asked.

"Sorry about that," she said, coming on clearer. "I was pulling off my dress."

Giving a mock whimper, Dylan plopped back on the couch and stretched out. Kayla wasn't helping. He could just see her pulling off one of her multicolored disasters to reveal the lush body he knew lurked underneath her horrible clothing. Kayla may not have an eye for fashion, but she'd caught his eye, and he hadn't been the same since.

Leaning back on the couch, he lightly scratched his hand down his flat stomach, which was sprinkled with light brown hair, and laid it loosely on top of his semi-erect cock. "Now you're just teasing me."

"No, if I wanted to tease you I would tell you about the pretty black lace panties I'm wearing."

This time he groaned for real, while rubbing his hardening cock through his boxers.

"Now, we're talking. What are you doing now?"

Laughing, Kayla replied, "I'm about to go to bed. Alone. Again."

"Well, you know that you going to bed alone is only by choice." Even though he said it in a joking manner, Dylan was serious. He had a soft spot for her in his heart and, because of her, a hard part several inches lower, all at the same time.

"You know what?" she joked. "One day you're going to say that one time too many and I'm going to take you up on your offer. Then where would you be?"

The image of Kayla straddling him immediately appeared in his head, causing his cock to harden further. "Hopefully underneath you, letting you work out some of your nervous energy."

"You make me feel good," she said, with a smile in her voice. "You're my best friend."

Groaning, Dylan let go of his cock. If there was anything that could still a hardening cock, it was being placed firmly back in the "friends only" category. "Now you've done it."

"What?"

"You've ruined my nap and my perfectly good erection," he moaned.

Amusement was evident in her voice when she said softly, "Good night, Dylan. Pleasant dreams."

"You're evil," he said as he hung up. Chuckling softly, he looked up at the ceiling, staring in her general direction. Taking another bite out of the apple, Dylan sat back down and groaned. "I might as well finish up," he muttered to himself, picking up a file.

Kayla let herself into Dylan's apartment the next day with a surprise for him in one hand and a cup of coffee in the other. Setting the black velvet bag on the kitchen counter, she headed towards his bedroom, where she heard him stumbling around. This was one of her favorite things about her days, beginning them with Dylan.

Working at home building web pages allowed her many luxuries, one of the big ones was her ability to start her day with Dylan. Making things was her first love, being with Dylan was her second. It had become a ritual of theirs a couple years back for Dylan to leave his door unlocked in the morning so she could slip in and chat while he got ready for work. They'd tried doing the whole emergency key thing, but Kayla couldn't keep track of her own keys and didn't want to risk losing one of his. Especially considering all the nice things he had in his apartment.

Dylan's apartment could have come out of a magazine. The curtains, the rugs and couches matched, with perfectly complimentary fixtures to tie in the room. It was an exact replica of his life, neat and orderly. His apartment was filled with tasteful, expensive, yet very comfortable furniture.

He liked everything to be in its place, but on the other hand, he wasn't afraid of a little mess. This was a good thing for Kayla who never met a dust bunny she didn't like.

She always joked with him that he kept her around to keep in touch with his inner child. Of course, he would mention she was childlike enough for the both of them.

Hearing him grumble, Kayla peeked her head in his bedroom and looked around the corner as she cheerfully greeted, "Good morning."

Dylan looked up from tying his tie and frowned. It normally took him a few hours just to get moving, and it seemed like today wasn't an exception. He wasn't a morning person. Hell, that was putting it lightly. Dylan was hardly an afternoon person, and nothing bothered him more than her cheerfulness first thing in the morning.

It took less than five seconds for him to take in her bright eyes and big smile before he grumbled, "I hate you."

Laughing, Kayla walked all the way in the room and leaned against his dresser. Placing the coffee on the dresser, she stepped in front of him and pushed his hands away. Taking his silk tie in her hands, Kayla started fixing it. "No, you don't."

That comment was as much a part of the ritual as the unlocked door. Dylan could never understand how she functioned on less than three hours of sleep. Her insomnia, which others might consider a burden, was what helped her when she worked.

Reaching around her, he grabbed the coffee cup and took a swig. Wincing at the bitter taste, he set it back down with a thump. Trying to push her away so he could finish the tie himself, Dylan and Kayla did a slapstick routine similar to an old episode of The Three Stooges for the rights to tie his tie.

"Your coffee sucks," he complained, as he gave up and let her finish.

"Aww, and I thought it was a vast improvement over yesterday's."

"Did you change the filter or the grounds?"

"No," she said, looking up at him with a puzzled look on her face. The idea of such a simple task never entered her mind. "I thought the machine made it really fast for some reason this morning."

Shaking his head in disbelief, Dylan moved her out of the way and gazed down to check his tie. Straightening it out, he glanced over at her with an indulgent look on his face. "I can read your future, Kayla, and it has food poisoning written all over it." With that parting shot, Dylan grabbed his suit jacket and his briefcase from his bed before heading down the hallway towards the kitchen, muttering to himself the whole way.

Laughing, Kayla followed behind him, drinking her coffee and watching the way his buns moved in his gray slacks. Even in his current state of grumpiness, Kayla had to admit Dylan was a very attractive man. Not flashy like today's movie stars, but more regal, like stars from the fifties. She teased him sometimes by calling him Cary Grant, because Dylan could wear a suit like it was painted on.

After setting the briefcase and his jacket on the coffee table, Dylan walked over to the door and opened it. Without a word of censure, he picked up the newspaper that she walked over before she came into his apartment. Shaking his head, he dropped the paper down on the table before reaching over and taking the cup out of her hands.

"Hey, I was drinking that," she cried, as he took the cup to the sink and poured the coffee down the drain.

"And your medical insurance will thank me later." Rinsing the cup, Dylan moved to his coffee machine and poured her a fresh cup of coffee from his maker.

"For your information I don't have medical insurance," pouted Kayla as she hopped onto the kitchen counter. She began to swing her legs back and forth, kicking them into his lower cabinets. Dylan stepped in front of her, raised his eyebrow, and handed her the steaming cup.

Kayla stopped kicking immediately. She knew her fidgeting bugged him, especially when she kicked his furniture. It was pure habit, nervous energy in motion.

"Sorry," she muttered, wrapping her hands around the warm cup, inhaling the strong aroma. Taking a sip, she looked up in surprise, "This is better."

"It's amazing what fresh grounds and a clean new filter can do."

Pouring himself a cup, Dylan leaned back against the counter and eyed her with a smile. "You look all dressed up this morning."

"I have a meeting with a client this afternoon."

"Really?"

"Yes, why?"

Dylan looked down at her clothes and burst into laughter. Following his gaze, Kayla grinned sheepishly when she noticed her outfit. She was wearing jeans that were ripped at the knees, not the fashionable expensive kind—but the honest-to-goodness ripped jeans from wear kind. She had on a loud orange shirt and her short hair was in two ponytails. She was barefoot as usual and if history was anything to fall back on, she probably looked like she had been up for hours.

"You know me. I'm all about dress for success."

Kayla let out a big yawn and set down her cup. Stretching her arms out to the side, she leaned her head back and gave out a big groan.

"Did you even try to go to sleep last night?"

"Nah," she said, swinging her foot back and forth. Dylan reached out and grabbed her leg, forcing her to stop. Sheepishly she grinned and replied, "I'll sleep when I'm dead. And besides at night is when I'm most creative."

"When was the last time you had a good night's sleep?"

Looking up as if lost in thought, Kayla squinted and pondered the question for a moment. "What do you consider a good night's sleep?"

"Uninterrupted seven hours or more kind of sleep."

"Okay, that's easy. The tenth grade."

Snorting, Dylan shook his head at her. "No wonder you're smiling all the time. You're wired."

"I am, aren't I?" Kayla agreed with a grin. "But last night it paid off."

"How so?"

"After talking to you, I was inspired."

"Inspired, huh?" he asked, his eyes gleaming. "Look, if it has anything to do with masturbation and Disneyland, I don't want to hear about it, unless you videotaped it and did a sexy voice-over."

He was such a tease. Dylan was always making comments about how sexy her voice was and if she thought for one minute he was serious, she would run full force and attack him. Kayla secretly wondered what Dylan would think if he knew he was the star of some of her late night self-love sessions. Probably die laughing, she thought with a grin. "Well, I guess you won't get to hear about it then."

"Please tell me I inspired you to go to Disneyland."

"No." Kayla just loved talking to Dylan. He had a dry sense of humor that always made her smile, no matter how terrible she was feeling.

"And you couldn't take time to pull out the video camera?' he asked, sounding hurt.

"No, I'm rewiring my camera. Remember?"

"What was your great idea this time, Professor?" Dylan teased, calling her by the nickname he gave her for her absentmindedness.

"When I got off the phone with you last night, I began to think of masturbation."

"Me too," Dylan mumbled.

"What?"

"Nothing, continue."

"And I started thinking of you and masturbation, and Eureka! It came to me." Kayla said, pointing to the black bag.

"What is it?" Dylan questioned warily.

"Open it up," she urged, dying to see his response. "It's my newest invention. I'm going to revolutionize the sex toy business."

"You're making a sex toy?" His voice thickened as he looked down at the bag in his hand.

"Yes," Kayla said. "I need you to help me test it out."

"Let me get this straight. You want me to help you with a toy?"

"Yes."

"What kind of sex toy is it?"

"An anal vibrator."

"You want me to use an anal vibrator on you?" A huge grin spread across his mouth as he opened the bag up and pulled out the anal plug.

"No, silly." Kayla laughed. "I want you to use it."

Confused, Dylan looked up and asked, "On..."

"On yourself, of course."

Chapter Two

Just when he thought Kayla couldn't do anything else to shock him, she would up and trump him. It was official. She had finally lost her fucking mind. Dropping the plug like it was a hot potato, Dylan looked at her as if she had two heads. "Did you fall and hit your head last night on the way to your worktable?"

"Of course not," Kayla said, jumping down off the counter and picking it up.

Examining the plug, she turned it over in her hand. Letting out a relieved sigh, she looked up and smiled. "You didn't break it."

"Well, give it to me and let me try again." Dylan felt nauseated. Just a few seconds earlier, he'd thought he reached the gates of paradise. Kayla, him and a sex toy. It was what the best wet dreams were made of. But instead of letting him relish in his naughty thoughts, she went and ruined it. Maybe if he closed his eyes, he'd wake up and realize it was all a dream—a horrible, twisted, deviant dream.

Kayla shoved the plug behind her back and frowned at him. "I spent all night working on this."

"Which is evident from the lack of sleep that must have gone into this hare-brained idea."

"It's not hare-brained. I did research and everything." Reaching into her back pocket, she pulled out some folded papers and waved them at him. "Look, it says right here that eighty-seven percent of men like having their prostate stimulated during oral sex."

"How many of those men are gay?"

"I don't know." Kayla shrugged.

"Well, go back and check your facts again, but this time use straight men."

Sighing, Kayla put her hands on her hips. "Dylan, straight men have prostates too, you know?"

"Show me a straight man who will let you shove that," he said, pointing to her crazy invention, "in their ass, and I'll show you a man who's really far in the closet."

"You don't know."

"And neither do you, Professor. But what I do know is you're insane if you think I'm going to let you shove a dildo up my ass."

"You say insane like it's a bad thing."

"When it involves my ass, it is." Moving back to his coffee machine, Dylan grimaced as he thought back to what she was trying to do. Just the thought of anything going near his ass was enough to make him wince. Kayla was going to be the death of him.

"I can't believe you're so upset about a little plug."

"I'm not upset, Kayla, I'm amused." And he was. Only

his little Professor would try to invent an anal sex toy. As far as Dylan knew, Kayla wasn't even into backdoor loving.

"Amused, why?"

"I'm amused you would even think I would do it."

"You didn't look amused to me." Tilting her head to the side, she smiled as she said, "I'd say more like neon green.

"Do you want me to kick you out?" Dylan growled jokingly. "And besides, if you're so cool with it, you use it."

"Dylan, I'm a woman." Kayla said it as if she were exasperated, which made Dylan want to chuckle. As if he could ever forget she was a woman. Even in the neon outfit from hell, her attributes were well pronounced.

"I'm very much aware of that."

"Well, in case you didn't know, women don't have prostates, therefore it won't work for me."

"What won't work?"

"The Walnut Wand."

What the fuck was that? "Walnut Wand?"

"Yes, this," she said, holding the plug towards him again. Dylan had to force himself not to jump back. He didn't want her waving the crazy thing around him.

"Kayla, let's say that even if I were a bit more open-minded, do you really think I would let you stick anything up my ass that you modified? The last time you talked me into allowing you to do something, you wired my computer to every appliance in my house."

"I was trying to make you more efficient."

"Kayla, I couldn't watch TV without my microwave going off."

"I fixed it, didn't I?"

"Don't you see? If you mess something like this up, you just won't be able to fix it. This is my ass we're talking about."

Kayla interrupted him with a sigh. "This time it's different."

"Really?" he asked, as he leaned back against the counter. Grabbing his coffee, Dylan settled back and watched her.

This should be great for a good laugh.

"How so, Professor?"

"I've been doing some reading online and…"

"Sure you did." He laughed. Knowing Kayla, she had mixed up her facts again.

"Just listen," she growled, squinting her eyes. "I've been doing some research on the male prostate and it's the size of the walnut, which is where I came up with the name 'The Walnut Wand', and it's supposed to be this big pleasure ball for men."

Shaking his head, Dylan set down his cup and looked at his watch. If he didn't cut this short, he would never get to work. Kayla would talk until doomsday to try to prove her point. "Kayla, I'm not letting you stick anything up my ass."

"I already have the prototype worked out. Basically I

25

just added a couple things to my butt plug."

"That's another thing I have to know," he questioned, completely sidetracked now. "Where the hell did you get a butt plug?"

"The same place I got my vibrator."

Eyes widening in shock, Dylan felt like he had been sucked into a vortex. This was unfreakingbelievable. Kayla had a vibrator. Dylan groaned at the mental image that swarmed through his head. His naughty little Professor pleasuring herself while he watched. Dylan instantly felt his cock stirring. Kayla and sex toy in the same sentence had a highly arousing effect on him. Closing his eyes, he tried to force his body to settle down. She was killing him. Literally killing him.

He didn't want to think about the fact that there was an anal plug less than two feet away from him. An anal plug that he could be using on his brown-haired vixen. Dylan could just imagine her turned around on all fours with the plastic, pink, love toy lodged in her ass as he pleasured her from behind.

Thoughts about Kayla and sex—or more to the point, sex with Kayla—were continuing to invade his brain of late. And maybe he wasn't the only who felt this way. He had begun to recently notice little things about her. If he didn't know better, he would think that they were in the beginning stages of flirting. Kayla was hugging him longer and touching him more, and god knows he was up for it. He had wanted her for a while now, but he didn't want to chance their friendship by making a play for her, but if she was up for it, then he sure in hell was.

"Is that a 'yes' groan or a 'maybe' groan?" Kayla teased, forcing a chuckle to escape from his tightly pressed lips.

"It's an 'I have to go to work before I do something that I'll regret' groan."

"Like saying yes?" she asked, hopefully.

"No, like throwing that pink demon in my garbage disposal." If he wanted to salvage their friendship and what was left of their sanity, he needed to get out of there before he put her little wand to some real use.

"Dylan!" Kayla cried, aghast.

"Kayla," he teased back. Walking out of the kitchen towards his bedroom, Dylan shook his head in amusement. Damn, she was cute. Even when she was threatening his manhood she was cute. Lethal and insane, but cute nevertheless.

There had to be a way to convince him to do it, Kayla thought as she tapped her finger against the plug. Maybe a trade of some sort. For heaven's sake, it was just a little plug. Sighing, Kayla brought it in for a closer inspection.

This really could have been a good idea. She just knew it was an untapped marketing niche. Kayla had been cruising adult stores for several weeks now, checking to see if there was anything out there like her idea, and although she had found several things close to her prototype, nothing worked like hers.

Well, at least she didn't think it did. The plug was actually a gag gift from her friend Missy who worked at Harris's Adult Books and Video store, and until now, it had sat in her drawer collecting dust.

Never having had anal sex herself, she wasn't sure of the purpose of one for a woman, but for a man it made perfect sense. It wasn't as if she had a walnut to experiment on, or she would use it herself.

Kayla thought for sure Dylan would at least consider using it. He was a healthy, sexually active man. He seemed very adventurous from the things he hinted at, so she didn't understand why he would say no to this.

"You've had anal sex before, haven't you?" she asked as soon as he came back into the room.

Dylan paused in mid-step and looked at her, sort of shocked. "Is nothing sacred?"

"Between friends, never."

"Yes, but as the pitcher, Kayla, never the catcher."

"You can't tell me you never had a woman stick her finger up your..." She demonstrated with her hand as she spoke, wiggling her finger about.

Dylan grimaced and shook his head as if trying to erase the image she was building.

"As a matter of fact, yes, I *can* tell you that."

"What if we use the unmodified one first, then work our way up?"

"Hell no!"

If anything the idea seemed to make him blanch.

Apparently that tactic was obviously not going to work. "I'm just asking for a favor," she tried, using a different approach.

"Collecting your mail when you go out of town is a favor. Taping a program on the VCR is favor. This, this is just craziness."

"What if I do something for you? I can update the computers for you at work or..."

Dylan's bark of laughter cut her off in midstream. "Not just no, but hell no. Kayla, you need to get some sleep because you've completely gone loopy."

"I'm just trying to help."

"And I understand that, baby. But there's nothing in this whole wide world that will ever convince me to use your device. When you make a blowjob wand, I'll be the first person in line for you to test it out on. In fact, I insist I be the only one."

"You're such a whore." Damn it, he was cute. Even when he wasn't doing what she wanted, Kayla couldn't get mad at him.

"And you're a menace with a screwdriver, but I still love you."

"Yeah, yeah, yeah." Sighing, Kayla didn't know what else to say. She didn't want to be annoying, but she had really hoped he would be more open to it. Seriously, she didn't see what the big deal was. All he would have to do is insert it and let her know what he thought. It couldn't take more than ten minutes.

"Look, Kayla, I know that you probably think right

now it's a good idea. But I'm sure with a Valium, some sleep, and years of therapy, you'll realize it wasn't."

Smiling, she shook her head. "Thank you for being so understanding."

"I'm trying to be. You know I'm always here for you. When you wanted to test out the new fire alarm you made, who went and bought all those extinguishers?"

"You."

"And when you caught on fire, who put you out?"

"Shut up!" Kayla said over his laughter. "You make me sound like Fire Marshall Bill. I didn't catch on fire. I got a little singed. But just like you're always there for me, I'll be there for you."

"Great, so if my asshole catches on fire, you'll put it out. That's very reassuring," he replied dryly.

"Come on, you know what I mean. Have you ever asked me to do something I haven't done?"

"I can think of one or two things."

"Like what?" Kayla asked. She knew she could be a tad demanding but she always thought she and Dylan had an equal relationship. He was so damn giving, at times she felt like he gave too much, but she had always tried her damnedest to be there for him as well.

"I seem to recall a phone call or two that left me high and dry."

"Come on, Dylan, you know you're only joking about that."

"Am I?"

That gave Kayla cause to pause. She had always thought that he was joking. What if he weren't? "Aren't you?"

Dylan didn't say anything for a couple of seconds. He just stared at her, forcing Kayla to really think back over his behavior, not that she needed much prodding. If for one second she thought he was for real, she'd be the first one naked.

"Of course I'm kidding," he said, ending the silence and her small ray of hope.

"I see how you are." Great, two dreams crashed in less than fifteen minutes. "Well, when I make millions on this, don't say I didn't offer to cut you in on the ground floor."

"Fine. When you're the Butt Wand Queen, I'll say I knew you when. I'll even help you invest it."

"Walnut Wand, thank you very much." Feeling dejected, Kayla placed the plug on his counter and plopped down on the stool. "Well, if you're not going to be my guinea pig, I guess I'll have to go find someone else."

"Good luck, Professor, but I have to go. We'll talk about this later."

"That's not a no."

"Dream on, Kayla," After putting on his jacket, Dylan picked up his briefcase and his keys.

They walked out the door together in silence, with Kayla headed towards the elevator as Dylan closed and locked the door behind them.

"Do you have your keys?" he questioned as he joined her at the elevator.

Kayla pushed the down button for him and leaned against the wall. Smiling, she nodded as she waited for the elevator to arrive. Dylan gazed at her with a knowing look until she reached inside her jeans' pocket and pulled them out.

"Sheesh," she muttered. "Lock yourself out of your own apartment a time or two—"

"Or nine?"

"Fine, *or* nine and people never let you hear the end of it."

"Sorry, Professor, I shouldn't have pigeonholed you like that."

"That's right," Kayla agreed, nodding her head. "Let's leave the past behind us."

"So, yesterday is the past?"

Damn it, she did forget yesterday, and of course Dylan hadn't. "It was yesterday, hello."

Realization dawned bright and clear in Kayla's mind at his laughter.

Dylan thought she was a complete scatterbrain. No wonder he wouldn't try her device. The only problem was she hadn't done much to prove him wrong.

Kayla was well aware of what people said about her behind her back, but it had never mattered to her because Dylan didn't care about those things. He was the one secure thing she had in her entire life, and she wasn't going to let a little wand come between them. "Are we still on for Friday night?"

"Yes, the guys will be here at seven sharp. Which means I'll call you at five and tell you the poker game begins at six."

"You act like I'm forgetful or something."

"Or something," he chuckled.

The elevator dinged its arrival and Dylan leaned over, giving her a quick kiss on the cheek before the doors opened. He stepped into the elevator and gave a polite nod to the elderly couple in the back

"Was that really a no?" she questioned once more as the doors began to slide together.

"It was a no," he said, firmly shaking his head.

Now what am I going to do? she thought, watching the door close with a frown.

That was really a no. Somewhere in the back of her mind, she had thought that Dylan would give in. He always had before. Maybe it was the laughter or the "hell no", but something about this time made her realize that he was for real.

Heading up the stairs, she lacked the usual spirit in her jaunt. Opening her unlocked apartment door, Kayla headed straight to her favorite room in the apartment, her office. It was the place that she spent the most time and the place she was most comfortable in. Her office was kind of like her mind, jumbled but filled with ideas, but no ideas stood out as much as the wand did.

It was everything an inventor could want, easy to make, easy to market and easy to sell. All Kayla needed now was a break and a willing ass. Setting the plug down on her desk, she pulled out her notepad and began to sketch ideas. She thought this was a good idea, but without a willing participant, she'd never really know. It wasn't like she could just pick up strange guys off the street and ask them to use the wand.

This is frustrating as hell.

Kayla leaned her head against her propped up fist as she contemplated her situation. This was it. Her penicillin. Her light bulb. Her blow up doll. The Walnut Wand was going to be her greatest invention yet, she just knew it.

Stop it.

Kayla sat up and set her shoulders back. She wasn't a quitter. The solution to her problem was so obvious, she felt almost moronic for not thinking of it before. If Dylan didn't want to use the wand that was fine. She'd just have to find someone else who would and Kayla knew the perfect person to help her with her quest.

Chapter Three

As Dylan set up the table for his monthly poker game, he watched Kayla across the room, flirting with his best friend and business partner, Chris Wilson. She had arrived on time for once, amazingly, and she looked fucking great.

Dressed in a short jean skirt and a black spaghetti-strap top, Kayla was playing up her advantage of femininity, or what she called her distracting factors, to a tee. Her brunette hair was styled in a sexy little bob, and unless he was imagining things, she actually had make-up on. Dylan was beginning to get really irked that she had gone out of her way to dress up for these bozos when he looked at her bright shirts and saggy sweats all week long.

Although he knew she was playing up her looks to take everyone's mind off the fact she was a card shark, it still really chapped his hide. Not that she was dressed up—Kayla looking mouth-watering was definitely something he could get use to—but because the little colorblind hellion had gotten dressed up for them.

He didn't like the way the other guys were looking at her, not that they were checking out her face much, just her lush cleavage and sexy legs. His cleavage and his legs, Dylan thought angrily as he yanked the legs up on the folding table. The same set haunting his dreams for the better part of a year.

"Hey, bud, we might need that leg," kidded his neighbor Dan from down the hall.

Dylan turned to make a comment but was brought up short by Dan, who was now turning his attention back Kayla's way. Dan was old enough to be Kayla's dad. Or at the very least her uncle and he had no right to be looking at her like she was an edible dish he couldn't wait to dive in.

He liked Dan, or he had until tonight, and Dylan would hate to have to kill him.

Wait! Why kill Dan when he could put them all out of their misery and take Kayla out? Yes, the idea of teaching the Professor a lesson wasn't a bad idea at all.

Dylan felt himself begin to calm down as he counted all the different ways in his head he was going to strangle and maim her. No, not strangle, spank. Spank would be more rewarding in the end. And the way he looked at it, Dylan had several reasons to dole out a punishment.

First, Kayla hadn't called him last night or come over in the morning like she usually did. To make matters worse, she didn't call him once during the day. Not one freaking phone call all day. She hadn't called to give him an update on her toy. There had been no emergency he had to help fix. No nothing.

And it really bothered him.

It wasn't like them to go a day without talking, and part of him was worried he might have hurt her feelings by not supporting her newest project. Not that he had changed his mind about being her crash-test dummy, but Dylan thought he might have handled it a little better.

After work today, Dylan stopped by her apartment to check on her, and she wasn't home. He had even let himself in with his key to check if she was ignoring him, and to his relief, she really wasn't there, but then that brought up a whole new set of questions.

Like, where the fuck was she?

Dylan didn't know how much it bothered him when she wasn't around, until she wasn't around. So much of his time was spent talking to her, or about her, he didn't know what to do when there wasn't anything to talk about or anyone to talk to. It wasn't until she didn't show up that he realized how much he'd come to treasure their time together. Almost as if he had taking her for granted, and that wasn't a feeling that sat well with him.

For a while he had thought it was just his attraction to her and their friendship that made him want to be with her, but then he realized it was something else.

He liked the fact that Kayla needed him. He actually took pleasure from knowing he was the first person she called when something good or bad happened. It made him feel needed and important to her, so much so that when she didn't call, he didn't know how to feel about it.

All this time he had thought it was she who needed him, but now he was really beginning to wonder if it wasn't the other way around and he who needed her.

It was a harsh reality to take in. And just when he was beginning to beat himself up for his selfish ways, Kayla showed up at his apartment, out of the fucking blue, like nothing was out of the ordinary.

It was as if the fact they hadn't talked all day didn't bother her as much as it had bothered him. With a box full of hot chicken wings and a pocket full of cash, Kayla had just strolled in and made herself at home in his apartment and with his friends. Showing off *his* goods.

"Let's saddle up, fellas," Samuel, another player, said to the scattered players in the apartment.

Kayla walked over to the table with one hand on Chris's arm, smiling, and it was enough to get Dylan's blood boiling. Before he could rationalize in his mind what he was doing, Dylan grabbed her other arm, and said over his shoulder, "We'll be back in a moment, guys."

Without waiting for a reply from Kayla or anyone else, he tugged her to the back of the apartment to his bedroom, with vengeance on his mind.

Shutting the door behind them, he leaned back and crossed his arms across his chest waiting for her to explain herself.

Looking bewildered, Kayla frowned as if she too were waiting for something. When Dylan didn't say anything for awhile, she finally spoke. "What's going on?"

As if she didn't know. "You tell me."

"Tell you what?" Kayla mimicked his stance, crossing her arms under her breasts, causing the luscious mounds to rise. "You're the one who dragged me back here."

"Where have you been all day?" he demanded, walking closer to her. Stopping directly in front of her, Dylan bent down and tugged on the bottom of her short skirt. "And what's with this get-up?"

"I've been out working on my project, not that I have to explain myself to you, bub, and for the record, you've seen this skirt a million times before. In fact, I wore it last week when we went out to lunch."

"What proje...the butt plug?" he questioned loudly.

"Walnut Wand, and keep your voice down," she whispered, looking over his shoulder at the closed door. "I don't want anyone getting wind of it until I've had it patented."

Was she kidding? Shaking his head in disbelief, Dylan leaned in closer and lowered his voice. "I don't think you're going to have to worry about someone trying to steal your anal idea."

"You never know."

"I'm pretty sure it's safe, especially from those guys," he said, gesturing over his shoulder. "Unless you know something about them that I don't."

"Of course not. Don't be silly."

"Speaking of silly, I think you should back off of Chris." Dylan couldn't help the jealous tone entering his voice. If anyone was going to benefit from her excess of energy, it was going to be him.

"Excuse me?"

"Chris comes with a lot of baggage. Hell, we've been friends for close to eight years and there are still things about him I don't know. Chris never gets too involved or stays with one woman for too long." *And you deserve better than that*, he added silently to himself.

Instead of looking as if she was heeding his warning, Kayla appeared amused. "I'm not interested in Chris, Dylan. I was just being friendly."

"Well, stop it."

"Make me."

Dylan's palm itched to do exactly that. The dare in her teasing tone was too much, especially with the way he was feeling right now. He'd sooner pull up her tiny excuse of a skirt and paddle her ass than let her walk back out there and fawn over Chris again.

Kayla was treading on dangerous grounds right now, and she didn't know what she was getting herself into, with Chris or with him.

"Come on," Kayla said, tugging on his arm. "Let's just get the game started. This isn't an eighteen-hour bra. It's a wonder bra, and it's squeezing the bejesus out of the twins."

Dylan wasn't appeased, but short of doing exactly what he wanted, he had no other choice but to follow her. Watching her walk out the door was the highlight of his day though. Her full, round ass swayed and the skirt clung to her like a second skin. Feeling his body beginning to respond to the sight of her soft delectable rear, Dylan quickly thought of all things not erotic to try to clear his head.

Baseball, the smell of the men's bathroom, her cooking. Anything to get his mind focused before his money wasn't the only thing he lost this evening.

Taking a seat at the table, Dylan looked around at his friends, who were all glancing not so subtly at Kayla's pale cleavage, and cleared his throat. When everyone glanced his way, even an amused Kayla, he muttered, "Ante up."

Kayla's winning streak that night had more to do with her bra than her brains. Every time she was backed into a corner, she would lean forward and squeeze her arms together, causing her breasts to swell and appear as if they were going to pop right out of her shirt.

Her only real competition that night was Dylan, who was onto her, but unfortunately, it didn't stop him from making a couple of bad moves either. All in all, she thought the twenty-dollar push-up bra had been a wise investment. It doubled her pocket in just one night. *This bad boy,* she thought amusedly, *is getting hand-washed and placed in a position of honor in the drawer.*

Racking up her loot, she nodded and smiled as the guys made their way out Dylan's door. As the last sucker, as she referred to them in her mind, left, she let out a loud cackle that would have done the evilest of witches proud.

"I kicked ass tonight," she roared as she jumped up from the table. "Go, Kayla, it's your birthday. Go, Kayla, it's your birthday."

"You are a grifter," muttered a disgruntled Dylan as he slumped onto his couch.

Kicking his shoes off, he put his feet on the coffee table. Leaning back with his arms folded across his chest, Dylan watched with an obvious smirk as Kayla did her victory dance.

Wiggling her hips and shimmying her breasts, Kayla slinked around in circles.

Rubbing the cash over her chest, she laughed at his disgruntled look and flaunted the money in his face. Winning was great, being able to throw it in Dylan's face was priceless.

"Men are such idiots," she said, throwing her head back and tossing the money in the air. The money showered over her like green confetti as it floated to the ground, landing at her feet in a puddle. Smiling, Kayla walked around the table and dropped down next to Dylan on the couch.

"Breasts are the best thing that God invented," she teased, laying her head on his shoulder. Rubbing against his neck like a kitten, she burrowed closer to him and inhaled his scent. A mixture of spicy cologne and aftershave lotion, Dylan smelled just like a good man should, intoxicating. It was a scent she couldn't get out of her mind.

Snorting, Dylan pushed the table forward and brought his legs to the ground.

Nudging at her with his shoulder, he tried to dislodge

her head.

"What, the poor baby upset that he lost to a woman?"

"I didn't lose to a woman," he scowled. "I lost to a pair of tits."

Gasping in mock outrage, Kayla poked her fingers into his ribs and wiggled them.

Knowing that Dylan hated to be tickled, she attacked him with relish. Groaning, Dylan grabbed her hands and fought off her advances. They wrestled, rolling onto the floor in their attempt to be the victor. Kayla landed on her back with Dylan firmly encased between her thighs and her arms held above her head in his strong grasp.

All laughter ceased to exist as they became aware of their potentially awkward situation.

"Just admit it," Dylan said softly. "You used your tits to unfair advantage."

"I didn't force anyone to look."

"As good of a player as you are," Dylan paused to glance down at her heaving breasts, "you wouldn't have gotten as lucky as you did if it weren't for these beauties. You used them to distract us. Admit it."

So he thinks the girls are beauties, huh? Kayla's breathing slowed as her arousal rose. The feel of Dylan, heavy and hard on top of her, was having a dangerous effect on her ability to think. She had to admit, it was a feeling she could grow to love.

"Maybe a little." Sliding her tongue over her parched lips, Kayla moved a little, forcing her skirt to rise higher on her hips and causing Dylan to shift directly between her thighs. The obvious sign of his arousal was pressed firmly against the moist juncture of her center.

Now this is certainly a very interesting development.

"Care to get up?" she asked, half-hoping he didn't. Kayla had been wanting him in this position for a while now and wanted to savor every second of it.

Pressing forward a little, he replied, "Not especially."

That works for me. Dylan's weight, full and strong, felt more than just right pressed against her. It felt damn good. So good in fact, that Kayla had to resist undulating her hips towards him. "Are you willing to put your money where your mouth is?"

"You have all the money you're going to get from me tonight," he replied as he released her arms. Placing his arms on the side of her head, he pressed up and rose off her, giving Kayla an eagle-eye view of what she had felt moments earlier. *Not only does it feel good, it looks damn good too*, she thought as he offered her his hand, helping Kayla to her feet.

Pushing her skirt down, Kayla said, "We don't have to play for money."

Raising one eyebrow, Dylan looked intrigued. "What are we playing for?"

Kayla walked towards the table and leaned against it. "Anything you want."

"Anything?"

"Yes."

Dylan moved towards her slowly, with a slight smile tilting up the edge of his mouth. "Anything can be a dangerous wager."

"I'm in a dangerous mood," she taunted. His erection wasn't the only thing up tonight. So was her courage. "Not man enough to make it?"

"Darlin'," he drawled. "I'm more than man enough, and you're about to find out."

As they faced each other, desire trickled through the room, making it hard for Kayla to concentrate. Staring at his mouth, Kayla wondered what it would feel like pressed against her. But more importantly, she wondered why they had waited so long to act on the chemistry between them.

"One hand, winner takes all."

"No backing out," he demanded. "That's the rule, Kayla. Me, you, and a deck of cards. Whatever the outcome, the loser has to abide by the winner's wishes."

"Yes," she said hoarsely, hoping against hope his wish would have them doing things she wouldn't even be able to think about later without blushing. "What do you want?"

"A phone call," he said, giving her a knowing look. "There are things I want more, like your body under mine. But I'm willing to be a gentleman about this. I won't force you to sleep with me because of a bad hand, but before this night is over, Kayla, I will know what you sound like coming."

A phone call? Well hell, at least it was a step in the

right direction. "I accept."

"What about you? What do you want?"

"You, as my test subject." It was all or nothing, and if he accepted, Kayla planned to make it as enjoyable for the both of them as possible.

The smile that was forming on his lips quickly turned into a frown. "Hell no."

"I'll help distract you," Kayla walked to him and placed her hand on his erect cock.

His cock twitched at her touch. Wetting her lips, she looked down at the bulge she was holding and wondered if she would be the one who ended up distracted. "Remember, you only have to do it if you lose."

Grabbing her hand, Dylan forced it harder onto himself. "Then I guess I won't lose."

Releasing her hand, he walked around the table and sat down facing her. Kayla took the seat in front of him and shuffled the deck.

"One hand, five-card stud, jokers are wild," Kayla said, as she offered him the deck to cut.

Shaking his head, Dylan watched intently as she dealt out the cards. Picking them up, Dylan composed his features, not letting on what his hand held.

Kayla looked down at her hand and groaned to herself. She had absolutely nothing.

Her highest card was an ace, so technically she could deal herself four new cards and keep the ace, but she didn't want to play that way. Keeping the ace of hearts and the ten of spades, Kayla set down the remaining cards in her hand.

Looking up from her cards, Kayla noticed Dylan watching her with an intense look on his face. He was hard to read, but he did have a lot more to lose, she thought with a smile.

"How many do you want?" Kayla nervously tapped her toe to the ground.

"I'll take one," he said, sliding one card from his hand on to the table.

"One." Kayla gawked.

"One."

"Okay. Dealer takes three."

Dylan smirked as she picked up the three cards in front of her. Picking up the card, she added them one by one to her hand. A five of clubs, the ten of hearts, and the ace of diamonds. *Two pairs*, she thought excitedly to herself. She might just make out okay after all.

"Whatcha got?" she asked excitedly.

"Let's place them down at the same time," he said.

Nodding her agreement, Kayla counted aloud. "One, two, three."

They flipped over their cards at the same time. Kayla looked down at his cards and cried out in despair. Dylan had a queen of clubs and nines. Four of them. Looking up from his cards on the table to the look of triumph on his face, Kayla felt like she was about to have a heart attack.

Leaning backwards in his chair, Dylan smugly flicked

his cards closer to her as if daring her to inspect them. Glaring at them, Kayla stood up and stepped away from the table.

At a loss for words, Kayla just stood as if in shock. When she finally was able to get a hold of herself, she looked back up at Dylan who had stood as well and was now leaning against his bar. He was watching her intently and giving her an amused little smile. Raising one eyebrow, he reached over the side of the bar, picked up the cordless phone from off the charger and said, "Call me."

This is not happening, she thought in a daze, as she stared at a smirking Dylan. Kayla could tell by the intense look in his eyes he wasn't going to let her back down. No amount of pleading and begging was going to get her out of it. Turning away, she walked slowly to the door. Hoping against all hope he would call her back at any second and say never mind.

As Kayla put her hand on the doorknob, Dylan called out from behind her. "Kayla?"

Hopeful, Kayla turned around and smiled nervously. "Yes?"

"I want you to take off your clothes before you call me. I want you naked and ready by the time you dial my number." Dylan walked towards her slowly with a sexy smile.

Standing in front of her, nose to nose, he reached around her and pushed the door open.

They were standing so close to one another she could

feel his breath on the side of her face. Dylan turned his head until he was whispering in her ear, "I want you naked, wet and willing by the time you say hello, or else."

Lightly slapping her on the ass, he smiled wider as she gasped in surprise. Dylan placed his hands on her shoulders and turned Kayla back around until she was facing the open door. Giving her a gentle nudge out the door, Dylan shut it firmly behind her.

Kayla walked to the elevator in a daze. Of all the stupid things to do, she couldn't believe she had lost, but the worst part was it was her idea to make the damn wager.

She would have never brought it up if she thought for a second she was going to lose.

The stupid, arrogant part of her that always got her in trouble never thought she would lose, although another part of her had wanted to. This was all so crazy.

Even without the twins, she was normally a better player at poker than Dylan. Five-card draw was her game. Fuming, she punched the up arrow on the elevator. Usually she just took the stairs, but tonight she was going to take the longest route home.

The dinging of the arrival of the elevator woke her from her daze and she slinked in apprehensively. This all seemed like a good idea at the time, she thought for the hundredth time. She rode the elevator in silence, contemplating her situation, as it crept up the shaft to her floor.

Everything moves in slow motion when you're nervous,

she thought. The doors slid open and she walked out, heading towards her door. Entering her apartment, Kayla made her way through the living room and straight back into the bedroom.

Taking her shirt off, Kayla stood in front of her bed nervously. She couldn't believe this was really going to happen. Slipping out of her skirt, Kayla's mind was going a hundred miles per hour, thinking of all the good and bad things, mostly bad, that could come out of tonight.

Why couldn't they just have sex like normal people? Sweaty, loud, bondage sex. Nasty, I can't face myself in the mirror the next morning sex. *Not* phone sex.

What if she giggled?

What if he did?

What if it didn't turn him on like he thought it would? An even better question, why couldn't he just want to fuck her?

It wasn't like she didn't want him. Because she did, she thought, as she threw the now offensive, bad luck bra across the room. She wanted him more than she wanted a new Mac computer, but she was worried that if something went wrong, then they would lose the best part of their relationship—their friendship.

As she slid her panties off, Kayla's stomach flittered with butterflies. Part from nervousness, part from arousal. Kayla didn't know which sensation was the strongest.

A hodgepodge of emotions battled in her mind. Right or wrong, the desire to share something so intimate and seductive with Dylan overruled all forms of common sense.

Walking over to her nightstand, Kayla picked up the cordless phone and dialed Dylan's number. *Here goes nothing*, she thought.

Chapter Four

Dylan sat on his couch, drumming his fingers on the seat. He was already sporting an erection just from the thought of Kayla calling. He knew this was exciting for her too, he just hoped she would work up the courage to call.

Staring at the phone, Dylan estimated how long it would take for her to call. She had been gone less than five minutes, but it was plenty of time for her to get in her apartment and get undressed.

She isn't going to go through with it, Dylan thought disappointedly. He felt his desire ebbing, but he refused to allow Kayla to back out now. They were so close to something special here, and she was going to allow her fears to ruin it. Well, not if he had anything to say about it.

Standing up, Dylan headed to the front door, just as a ringing noise came from the couch. Smiling slowly, Dylan walked over and answered the phone.

"Hello."

"Dylan?"

Dylan could hear the question in her voice. Wanting to alleviate her fears, Dylan tried to calm his erratic heartbeat and speak to her in a soothing voice.

"Yes," he replied as he sat back down.

His erection had jumped back to life as soon as the phone rang. It was amazing how clairvoyant his penis was.

"I feel silly doing this," Kayla whispered.

"Don't back out now, Kayla."

"It feels weird."

"Nothing can be weird between us, baby. Just go with it. Let your inhibitions go."

"'Kay," she said nervously.

Dylan unbuckled his belt with one hand, while gripping the phone tightly with the other. He couldn't believe his fantasy was finally going to come true. Dylan stood up and unbuttoned his pants with haste.

Walking down the hallway to his bedroom, Dylan pressed his ear harder to the phone, trying to ensure he heard every sound she made. Entering his room, he pulled the phone away, tugged his shirt off and quickly brought the phone back up to his ear.

Dylan pushed his pants along with his boxers to the ground, his member standing out thick and hard in anticipation. He made his way over to his nightstand and opened up the top drawer to extract the oil he kept there for extra lubrication. Pressing the phone between his shoulder and his ear, he dribbled a little oil into his palm and sat down on the bed.

All the while he readied himself, Kayla hadn't made a sound. It was a first for his mile-a-minute baby. She must have been more nervous than he thought.

"You still with me?"

"Yes."

"Good." Propping the plush pillows behind his back, Dylan brought his legs onto the bed, dropping one flat and leaving his other leg bent at the knee. Gripping his cock tightly in his hand, he settled back. "Where are you?"

"In my bedroom."

"Did you get undressed like I asked?"

"Yes."

"Good," he said, stroking his erection. "Go stand in front of your mirror."

There was a shuffling noise and Dylan heard a door shut. He knew that Kayla's full-length mirror was on the back of her bedroom door. Dylan closed his eyes and imagined her there in front of it.

"Tell me, what do you see?"

"I see me."

"Describe yourself to me," Dylan demanded as he ran his thumb across the wet head of his throbbing cock.

"Dylan, you know what I look like."

"I don't know what you look like naked."

Her frustrated sigh resonated over the line, but Dylan wasn't going to allow her to give up that easily. "I'm waiting, Kayla."

"I see my breasts."

"What do they look like?"

"They're full and heavy." Her voice lowered. "And my nipples are hard."

That was just what he wanted to hear, but still, Dylan needed to know one thing. "Because of what we're doing or because it's cold?"

"Because of what we're doing," Kayla said softly.

"Touch them for me, baby."

"I am," she replied, her voice catching a bit at the end. "I'm rubbing them between my fingers and tugging on them."

"What color are they?"

"Pink."

There was a moment of silence as he envisioned her standing proudly and aroused in front of him.

"Are you hard, Dylan?" she questioned shyly.

"Honey, I was hard the minute you walked into my apartment this evening. I've wanted this for a long time, Kayla. To listen to you as I stroke myself. To hear your sexy little voice while I come," he said, running his hand down his length. "To hear you come, screaming in my ear."

Kayla let out a soft moan, which caused his cock to jump in response. Some things were truly worth waiting for.

"Lay down on the bed, baby, and spread your legs."

The rustle of the bed covers let him know she was complying with his wishes.

"Is this what you want, Dylan? Me touching myself as you listen."

"Yes," he said hoarsely. "Are you wet?"

"Very."

"I've been wanting you wet for awhile, baby."

"I never knew. Not wanting to sound too clichéd at this moment, but you had me at hello." She gave a husky little laugh. "I've wanted you since the first day I saw you."

"What are you doing now?"

"I'm running my fingers through my pubic hair, lightly touching my lips."

Dylan's mouth suddenly went dry. Licking his lips to moisten them, he cleared his throat. "Can you feel how wet you are?"

"Yes, you have me flowing," she panted into the phone.

Squeezing his aching cock, Dylan imagined Kayla in her bedroom, stroking her fingers over her pussy. Tightening his hand, he asked a question he had being dying to know for a while. "What do you taste like, angel?"

"I...I don't know."

"Taste yourself for me."

"'Kay," she whispered.

The silence that ensued damn near drove him mad. "Tell me."

"I...I taste...Dylan, I don't know what to say. I've never

done this before."

"Sure you do, angel, just tell me what you taste like. Slip your finger deep inside of your pussy and swirl it around, until you're coated from tip to knuckle. Then I want you to bring your hand up to your luscious mouth and taste yourself. Lick your cream from your fingers, much the way I want to.

"Tell me now, Kayla."

"I taste good." Her voice broke a bit as she spoke. "Rich, tangy even, but a bit sweet."

Dylan could almost taste her himself. "I bet you do, baby. I bet you do. I bet that pretty pussy of yours is as delectable as the rest of you. If I were there right now, I'd be down on my knees in front of you. Tasting you, burying my face is your sweet honey. Drowning in your juices. I'd make you come over and over again, just from my mouth alone."

Whimpering, she let out a little moan, causing Dylan's cock to ache in response. Apparently he wasn't the only one getting off on his little fantasy.

"What are you doing?" he asked breathlessly. Slowly pumping himself, Dylan ran the heel of his hand over the head of his cock, bringing the lubrication from the oil down farther onto his member.

"I'm caressing myself," she breathed into the phone, breathlessly. "Touching my outer lips, gliding my fingers across my clit." Moaning louder, she uttered, "Sliding my fingers inside..."

Unable to finish the sentence, Kayla's cries of passion

resonated through the phone lines, making the hairs on the back of Dylan's neck rise. Her voice, calling out to him, sent shivers of desire coursing along his body.

He could tell she was getting closer by the choppy sounds she was making in his ear.

Dylan picked up his tempo and felt the familiar tug on his testicles. This was better than he could have ever imagined. Kayla coming. Kayla coming for him, moaning his name, made his gut clench. Her passion fueled his own, making every stroke more maddening than the one before.

He fucked his fist, wishing it was her pussy surrounding him, wishing, with everything inside him, he was upstairs pounding into her instead of one floor below, listening to her whimper with need. Just when he was close to reaching his peak, Kayla cried out his name as she came.

"Fuck this," he muttered, clicking the phone off and dropping it onto the bed.

Grabbing his sweats out of his bottom drawer, Dylan pulled them over his throbbing cock. His balls ached for relief, but he could walk, just barely. Without putting on a shirt or shoes, Dylan grabbed his keys and slammed out his apartment.

Taking the stairs two at a time, Dylan groaned in agony as his unfulfilled cock pulsated in pain. When he reached her floor, he stormed to her door, unlocked it and slammed the steel behind him.

Feeling like a man possessed, Dylan flung his keys on

the floor and strode down her hall. Kayla was standing in her bedroom doorway, pulling her robe on. She held the phone in one hand as she tried to gather the robe together with the other.

"What's wrong?" she questioned as he stopped in front of her. "It wasn't working for you?"

Not working? He'd had intercourse that had left him less satisfied than their few minutes on the phone.

Taking the phone from her hand, Dylan let it clatter to the floor as he grabbed her hand in his. He lifted her still-moist fingers into his mouth and tongued her essences. The tangy flavor of her sex mingled with the spicy aroma of her arousal sent pulsating shivers down his body.

Letting her fingers slowly slide from his mouth, Dylan looked into her passion-filled eyes as he slid her robe down her shoulders onto the floor.

Dylan watched the garment as it fell down her body, revealing every inch of her lovely form. Kayla was everything he thought she would be and more. Embarrassment shone from her skin, leaving it tinted red as she made to cover herself.

"Don't," he said huskily. "Don't be afraid of me."

"I'm not afraid," she denied. "I thought it was just going to be phone sex."

"Did you really think I would be satisfied with just listening to you come? When I can be here, inside you, making you come?"

Dylan stepped forward, forcing Kayla to move

backwards into her bedroom. His intense stare never left her face. "Do you have anything? I left the apartment in a bit of rush."

"I'm on the pill."

"Good," he said, leaning down to kiss her. "Just so you know, I'm fine. I had a physical last month, so you have nothing to worry about from me."

"Or me," she whispered as his lips gently brushed hers.

"Baby, the only thing about you I'm worried about is if I'll fit inside your tight little body. Anything else is of no importance."

Bending down, Dylan moved in closer to deepen the kiss, but Kayla backed away a bit and pushed her hand against his chest to ward him off.

"I have a request."

"Just one? I'm willing to do anything to you that you want. Whatever turns you on turns me on. I just want to hear you scream my name."

His words sent tremors down her body.

Wetting her lips, Kayla desperately tried to rein in her desire. At the rate he was going, she was going to dissolve into a puddle right in front of his eyes. She had never been this aroused in her entire life. Dylan had done more to her with a few simple words than her few boyfriends had done with their entire bodies.

This man was lethal.

Clearing her throat, Kayla said breathlessly, "There has to be another night."

Confusion flashed across his face. "What do you mean?"

"I know how you are, Dylan," she said, holding up her hand to stop any further comments he might have made. "You lose interest real quick, and I refuse to be a one-night stand."

Frowning in irritation, he pushed her down on the bed and knelt before her. Looking at her full breasts, he reached out his hands and cupped them. He took his time familiarizing himself with her breasts before bringing his face forward and taking an erect nipple in his mouth.

He toyed with her. Teasing her as he alternated between sucking motions and soft biting. In less time than it took for her to mutter his name, Dylan had her creaming and soaking her bedspread again.

Moving his hand down her body, he slipped his fingers between her folds and caressed her engorged clit.

Arching her back, Kayla swiveled her hips as Dylan fingered her. His touch was like fire to her already over-inflamed skin. Unable to help herself, Kayla gyrated herself on his fingers. Her body racing quickly towards another orgasm as if the first one had never occurred.

Dylan released her taut nipple and caught her passionate gaze with his. "If you think I'm going to be happy with only one more time after this, then you're crazy."

As if she could think at a time like this.

He slid his fingers out of her soaked pussy and brought them to his mouth. As he held her gaze, Dylan cleaned his fingers of her cream before sitting up. Only the sound of their breathing could be heard as he spread her legs farther apart and pulled her hips forward so that her bottom was almost hanging off of the bed.

No words were needed. Kayla was ready for him to finish with his tongue what he'd started with his fingers. More than ready.

When Dylan placed her legs over his shoulder and took her pulsing pussy in his mouth, Kayla thought she'd died and gone to heaven. His tongue, his lips, pleasured her like no one ever had before. Dylan was a patient lover. He feasted from her as if she held the fountain of youth between her thighs.

Patient yes, gentle no. He possessed her mound like a man on mission. Separating her lips, Dylan firmly licked up one side of her pussy and down the other. Teasing her, he ignored her clit. Instead he licked her lips, stopping to tug gently on the soft, light brown, downy hair that felt like peach fuzz around her pussy.

It was too much, yet not enough, all the same time. She needed more. Kayla lay back on the bed and tried to scoot back, but Dylan stopped her by holding her legs tight.

Burying his mouth further against her pussy, Dylan flicked her clit with his tongue in rapid succession before finally taking the heated button in his mouth and sucking it. Kayla arched her back and dug her heels into his flanks. Twisting from side to side, Kayla tried to jerk away from the pleasure-pain radiating from her center, but Dylan held tightly to her thighs as she came, shaking around him.

Moaning and arching, Kayla rode the orgasm washing through her like a tidal wave. The intense pleasure felt as if it would burn her alive. It was too much, too powerful for her to take in just one sitting and yet it seemed as if Dylan wasn't ready to stop just yet.

"Dylan please, I can't take anymore. I...I..." Kayla begged, as she tugged at his hair.

Ignoring her, Dylan just grunted and moved his tongue in small circles inside her, licking, drinking from the fountain pouring out of her, like honey from a hive. Shaking and shivering, she slowly began to calm down as Dylan slowed down his strokes.

Just when she thought she couldn't take the pleasure any longer, Dylan pulled back slightly and blew cool air on her clit, causing her to cry out again. The contrast between the fire of her pleasure and the cool winds of his breath made her pleasure ten times as intense.

Dylan paused in his sensual torment of her and pulled back for a few seconds, letting Kayla calm down before leaning forward again and attacking her clit with his tongue once more. Groaning, Kayla tried to pull him away, but Dylan grabbed her hands from his head and held them down by her side as he licked her into another mind-blowing orgasm.

As she shuddered in the aftermath, goose bumps

broke out over her damp skin.

Breathing heavily, Kayla lay limply as Dylan rose from between her legs and pulled his sweats down past his bulging erection.

Kayla's eyes widened and she licked her parted lips as she got her first glimpse of his dick. He was long, thick and hard. The purplish mushroom-head of his cock was glistening with pre-cum, giving it a sexy glow.

Taking his cock in his hand, Dylan pumped it a few times while watching her on the bed.

"You taste better than I ever could have imagined," he said, as he climbed on the bed beside her. Scooting to the top of the bed, Kayla sat up and took his cock in her hand. She leaned forward as if to take it into her mouth, but Dylan placed his hand on her shoulder and held her back.

"I don't think so, love." He chuckled. "I won't last long inside that hot fucking mouth of yours."

"Get inside me," Kayla whimpered. "I don't care where, but now."

"That is a very dangerous offer, baby. There are lots of places my cock would just love to be. Places that would fit it like a glove, so be careful what you ask for."

Ask! At this rate, she was willing to beg.

Leaning over, he took her mouth with his. Kayla could taste herself on his lips and tongue as he lapped at her. Pushing her back on the bed, Dylan shifted her while never taking his mouth from hers. He placed his hand under her leg, raising it higher as he laid his other palm down flat on the bed next to her hip.

Kayla closed her eyes as she felt the head of his cock at the entrance of her pussy.

Kayla felt a slap against her clit. Opening her eyes, she saw Dylan with his cock in his hand. She couldn't believe it. He'd just spanked her clit with his dick.

"Now that I have your attention again," he said dryly.

"What?"

Pushing his cock inside of her, he slid forward, lifting her leg to the top of his shoulder as he leaned over her. Kayla shut her eyes again, arching in pleasure as he pulled out and pressed in again.

"No, Kayla," Dylan said roughly, as he plunged in deeper. "Keep your eyes on me...only me."

"I can't..." she whimpered as he moved in her.

"Oh, but you will if you want me to fuck you. I want there to be no doubts as to who is inside you. I want you to know it's my cock you're taking."

Opening her eyes, Kayla watched Dylan's face as he fucked her. He stared down into her eyes as he plunged in and out. Only slowing down to shift her leg as it slid down his sweat-glistened arm, Dylan never lost eye contact. He was deep inside her, pushing her across the bed as he thrust within her.

Reaching up, Kayla grabbed the headboard to stop it from banging into her head. Her pleasure-pain sensor was off the chart as he drove deep into her soaking flesh. Sliding his hands under the small of her back, Dylan propelled her back against him, forcing her to give as good as she was getting. For every thrust he gave her, she pushed back into him, pushing him further into the recesses of her body, until the tip of his thick cock brushed against her cervix, causing her to come, screaming his name.

"God yes," he moaned against her neck. "Fuck, baby, come for me."

Twisting underneath him, Kayla fought the pleasure until it overtook her, causing her to cry out and let go of the headboard. Wrapping her arms around him, she marked him with her nails as she dragged them down his back.

"Fuck me, fuck me," she chanted over and over again, as he powered into her.

Picking up speed, Dylan drove into her with all his might. "I'm coming."

Crushing his hips into hers, he threw his head back and moaned as he came, spilling his seed into her. Leaning forward, he rested his head beside her while holding himself up on shaky arms.

Kayla lay as if in a daze with her arms still wrapped around his wet, quivering body. She was completely amazed. She had never had three orgasms in one night, ever. Lying down on her breasts for a second, Dylan turned his head and blew on her softening nipple. It jerked in response, which caused his cock to twitch inside her.

"No...you've got to give a girl a moment," she

whimpered, turning his head away from her nipple. "Get out of me."

Chuckling, Dylan rose up and pulled his hips down, dislodging himself from her. He groaned as he rolled over onto his back and lay next to her. His limp cock, still impressively thick, left a trail of moisture between her legs.

Looking down, Dylan winced. "You have something I can clean up with?"

"The shower."

"Darling, I barely have enough energy to wipe, let alone move my tired ass all the way to the shower."

"Well, I guess you do deserve something for all your hard work," she teased, as she leaned over the side of the bed and picked up a discarded shirt she had on the floor.

Dylan cleaned himself and then folded the shirt in two before slipping it between her legs.

Looking down, Kayla watched through half-closed eyes as Dylan wiped away all traces of his semen from her legs.

"You know, Dylan," she said, turning her head on the pillow until she faced him. "If I had been aware that you were that skilled five years ago, I would have called you collect."

Laughing, Dylan leaned over and kissed her softly on the lips. Kayla faintly smelled her essence on him, but the rest of the sexual aroma lingering in the air overpowered the faint smell of her. She took his tongue in her mouth and caressed it with her own.

Breaking the kiss, Dylan brought his hand up to her face and gently cupped her cheek. "If I would have known you tasted that good, I would have been eating all of my meals from between your legs."

Kayla blushed, which caused Dylan to burst out in laughter. "How can you still blush after what we just did?"

"It's because of what we just did I'm blushing. I would have never thought you were such a potty mouth."

"I do believe it was you screaming 'fuck me, fuck me'."

"Shut up," she said, rolling onto her stomach and burying her face in her pillow. "I did not."

"Oh yes, you did, my little fuck-baby. That was you who demanded I fill you," Dylan paused to run his fingers down the line of her back to the crack of her ass, "in any place I wanted."

Tightening her buttocks, she rolled back around, bringing the pillow with her and lightly smacking him in the head. Getting up on her knees, she attacked him with glee. Howling with laughter, Dylan dodged the pillow as she pummeled him with blows.

"Shut up. Shut up. Shut up," she said, between laughter and swings. It was one thing to say those things in the heat of passion and quite another for him to bring it up when she was sated.

Grabbing the pillow from a laughing Kayla, Dylan threw it out of the way before bringing her down for a hard kiss. Their laughter ceased to exist as they explored each other's mouths. Pulling away reluctantly, they looked into each other's eyes.

"Dylan?"

"Yes, baby."

"I don't want this to ruin our friendship." It was her biggest fear. In the back of her mind, Kayla had always known sex with Dylan would be spectacular, but even mind-numbing orgasms weren't worth a hill of beans if they meant losing Dylan as a friend. His friendship was irreplaceable and she'd hate to lose it because of one night of bliss. "You're the most important man in my life and I would hate for anything to come between us."

Dylan glanced down between their bodies at his stiffening erection and back at Kayla with a slight smile. "Well, I can pretty much promise you he'll come between us from time to time, but nothing is more important to me than us being friends."

"I just don't want things to change." Sitting up, Kayla looked at him worriedly. "I hate change."

"Life is full of change, Professor," he said, sitting up so he was at her level. "But change isn't always bad, and I can never go back to being just your friend, and neither could you. This is something so much better than simple friendship."

"But friends foremost, right?"

Smiling at her, Dylan ran his fingers across her cheek, causing her heart to skip a beat. Leaning forward, he gently kissed her on the tip of her nose like he used to, and suddenly, everything felt right in her world. "Friends."

Chapter Five

Great sex was an amazing mood-altering drug. Normally Dylan abhorred Monday mornings, but today was unlike any of its evil predecessors. This was the Monday after spending the weekend making love with Kayla.

Dylan couldn't help the extra pep in his step as he strolled through the doors of his office building. He was in a great mood. Saying hello to everyone he passed, he smiled brightly and winked at his scowling secretary, Mrs. Howard, as he entered his office. Today, not even her sour disposition was enough to bring him down. Not after the weekend he'd just spent with Kayla.

Who would have thought they would have had such a great time together? Not him, that was for sure. Although looking it back, it should have been obvious. With as much fun as they had together with their clothes on, it should have just went to reason they would have even more fun with them off.

Just thinking Kayla's name brought a smile to his face. For more than one reason, because not only was she the best friend he'd ever had, but also the best piece of ass he had ever had.

She was willing, limber, and very, very accommodating. Kayla wasn't too shy to try things, to suggest things, or to be assertive and take charge in the bedroom. It was a refreshing change from the previous women in his life, who didn't want to appear to be too bawdy. Kayla just didn't care. If she wanted something, she asked for it. No, she demanded it.

He almost had a heart attack when in the middle of doggie-style, Kayla asked him to spank her. It had taken all of his hard-won control not to come inside of her right then and there.

Of course, Dylan had been more than happy to comply, and when he came, he damn near put his back out. Jokingly, Dylan had stated he hadn't had that much sex since college, which brought out Kayla's competitive side and if it wasn't for liniment and the sauna in the tub, neither one of them would have been walking the following morning.

Last night, in an attempt to get some rest, they had agreed to sleep alone. It was the first time since Thursday night Dylan had actually gotten any sleep, only to be awoken this morning by her mouth on his cock. For once, her insomnia paid off.

A blowjob was the best possible way to start a day.

Sitting behind his desk, Dylan looked through the mail Mrs. Howard had dropped in front of him before demanding if he wanted a cup of coffee.

"That would be lovely," he replied, handing her his cup.

Grabbing it, she stomped, as was her way, out of his office, almost running headlong into Chris, who rolled his eyes as she grumbled at him for being in her path. Chris ignored her, as they all did when she was in one of her moods, and continued into the office as if she hadn't spoken. It was so out of the norm for Dylan to be in a good mood so early in the morning, and especially on a Monday, that when Chris neared him, he halted in his tracks.

"Either you've figured out some poor helpless soul you could pawn off Mrs. Howard on or you're coming up with ways to dispose of her body."

Laughing, Dylan kicked up his feet and leaned back in his chair. "Neither, my friend. I just had the best damn weekend of my life."

Smiling at Dylan's expression, Chris walked around and sat in the brown leather chair facing Dylan. "Give me details, man, and don't leave anything out. I want sight, smell, and sound."

"Well, a gentleman never tells."

"And when a gentleman comes in this room, I'll understand," snorted Chris as he slouched down in the chair. "But until then, spill it."

If it had been any other man, Dylan wouldn't have said a word, but Chris and he were more than business associates, they were best friends. Or as close to best friends as Chris would allow. Despite knowing each other for almost a decade, there was still a wall Chris kept between them. But the wall wasn't reserved only for Dylan, it was there for everyone, so Dylan had learned to accept it. Still, if there was anyone he would confide in, it was Chris.

"Let's just say I had a better time after the poker game than you did."

"Bullshit!" Chris sat up in surprise. "You and the Professor?"

Grinning, Dylan nodded. He would have said much more but Mrs. Howard came back into the room, halting all conversation. It was fine with Dylan though, because it gave him ample opportunity to study Chris's stunned face.

As if oblivious to the silence, Mrs. Howard placed his coffee on his desk and stood as stiff as a solider. "Don't forget you two have an eleven o'clock in the conference room."

Dylan nodded at her but kept his gaze focused on a shell-shocked appearing Chris. He laughed inside as he watched Chris try to pull himself back together. Their joint silence lasted as long as it took Mrs. Howard to huff from the room.

The second she passed through the door, Chris pounced. "The Professor, but she's so..."

"So what?" Dylan asked coolly.

As if noticing the change in Dylan's expression, Chris quickly backed down. "That's not what I mean, man, and you know it. I dig her, I do. I've always thought she was great. I'm just having a hard time imagining you two together. You're so...you, and she's so not you. She's a great girl, funny, sexy in a Rainbow Bright kind of way, but not your usual type."

Dylan burst out laughing at his description of Kayla. He couldn't help but understand Chris's surprised reaction. Even he was amazed at times at the change in their relationship, but it just felt right.

"Sometimes you have to go with what you feel and leave common sense out of it."

"Well, how did it feel?"

"Un-fucking-believable." Dylan grinned.

Chris waited a few seconds, but when Dylan didn't elaborate, he raised a brow questioningly. "Is that all the detail I'm going to get?"

"Yes."

"You fucking suck," he groaned.

"As does she," pausing for the dramatic, Dylan added with a huge grin, "very, very, very well."

"Now, now, now, gentlemen," said a slightly accented voice from the doorway. "Is that any way to talk about a lady?"

Dylan and Chris both jumped up at the sound of Eliza Rivera, Chris's secretary's voice. From the devilish tone in her voice and the sassy smile on her lips, Eliza had heard a lot more than Dylan would have liked.

He was so screwed. Hoping Chris had an idea on how to deal with this latest glitch, Dylan turned to his friend for help. But from the lustful look on his friend's face, he knew Chris wasn't going to be much help at all.

It wasn't as if he could blame Chris. In all things, Eliza was the complete opposite of his own secretary. Not only was she courteous, kind and a joy to work with, Eliza was a very beautiful woman. Exotic was actually the word for it, with long dark straight hair and big hazel eyes. She was built like the proverbial brick shithouse, full breasts with a full bottom, and from the way Chris watched her, Dylan knew his friend wanted her bad.

But she was Chris's problem. Dylan had his own troubles to deal with.

"Eliza," Dylan said, moving from behind his desk. "What she doesn't know won't hurt me."

Laughing softly, she walked fully into the room. "She who?"

"She nobody." Even to him, his comments sounded lame.

"Mmm, well, I hate to see a grown man cry, but I do have to look out for my girls." Looking coyly from beneath her full lashes, she turned on the charm as she slinked up next to Dylan. "Although I'm not above taking a bribe."

"Name it and it's yours," he joked in mock horror.

"Well, did I hear you correctly or did you two mention a poker game?"

"Yes, you did," replied Chris, coolly raising a black brow. "Why? Do you play?"

"I grew up with three brothers. There aren't many

games I don't play, and play well, I might add." Her last words were said like a challenge, and knowing Chris like Dylan did, it was probably a challenge he'd loved to take. "Do you need another player?"

"I don't know," Dylan said, crossing his arms. "We got pretty well duped by the Professor on Friday, so I'm not much on women players anymore."

"Is this Professor the one who gives good head?" Her tone was pleasant as she blackmailed him with a straight face.

Dylan knew when he was beat. "It's the first Friday of every month."

With a self-satisfied grin, Eliza turned to Chris and handed him his messages. "Would you like some coffee?"

"No." Chris was barely able to drag his eyes away from her breasts to answer coherently. "I'm fine."

"I'll be at my desk if you need anything." With a wave her hand, Eliza left the room, leaving the men staring in her wake.

As soon as she was completely out of sight, Chris plopped back in the chair and groaned, "Why?"

Had Chris missed the entire conversation? "You heard her, it was a do-or-die moment."

"I get enough of her around here," he said, lifting his head up and looking at Dylan. "And now you've invited her to our game."

"Why did you hire her if you can't stand being around her?"

"Because I listened to the little head, instead of the big head."

"It's not like she growls at you, like some people," Dylan said, gesturing with his head towards Mrs. Howard. The typing from the outer office suddenly stopped as if she heard them, then quickly resumed faster than before. Chris and Dylan both winced at the pounding of the keyboard.

And Chris thought he had it bad. To be so fucking unlucky.

Clearing his throat, Chris continued in a lower voice. "No, and she's a good secretary. She always brings me coffee, she smells great, remembers all my appointments and never complains when she has to work late."

Poor baby. Life was just so rough for some people. The more Chris complained, the less sorry Dylan felt for him. "So what's the problem?"

"Have you fucking seen her, or does a woman have to wear neon colors to get your attention?"

"Shut up." Dylan couldn't help but laugh.

"Seriously, man, it's hard to work around someone that fucking beautiful. I can't think, I can't work and she makes me feel like a blithering idiot."

"I'm sure that's not hard."

"Eat me." Chris shook his head as he stood. "I've got to roll, but I'll see you at the meeting in a few."

"Yeah, maybe we should take Mrs. Howard, instead of Eliza. I would hate for you to get too distracted."

"Fuck you," he mouthed at a laughing Dylan, before leaving his office.

With pen and notepad at the ready, Kayla pushed through the swinging red doors of Harris's Adult Books and Video store. Since her newest brainstorm, Harris's had become almost like a second home to her. She had spent all afternoon there on Wednesday, and damn near all day there on Thursday. And if it hadn't been for Dylan's most persuasive bedroom manner, Kayla would have more than likely spent all weekend here.

Although looking back on her weekend of bliss, Kayla had to admit she didn't miss working at all. There was just something about Dylan's brand of research that was very, very educational.

Just thinking back to their weekend together made Kayla's body tremble. Dylan had turned out to be everything she had always hoped for in a man, sexually, at least. For Kayla refused to think beyond the bedroom. They had a great friendship and they were dynamite together in bed. It was enough for her, despite what the little voice in her head kept whispering.

Kayla refused to listen to that voice. She wasn't going to let her overactive imagination, something she normally prided herself on, ruin what was happening between them. Besides, Kayla knew Dylan. She *really* knew him, and after five years of friendship, Kayla understood that the quickest way to run him out of her life was to push for a long-term relationship.

The fear of losing Dylan as her friend was almost as overwhelming as the fear of never being as happy as she had been this weekend in his arms. In some ways it made her regret the change they had embraced. Yet at the same time, Kayla knew she wouldn't trade what they had now for a billion dollars.

"Back so soon?"

Surprised out of her silent reverie, Kayla jumped at the sound of her friend, Missy Hadden, so close to her. She had been so deep in thought she never heard the smiling woman approach.

The two had met about a year ago when Missy's laptop had taken a dump on her and she'd brought it to Kayla to fix. She was a college student who worked at Harris's part time and the first person, despite her misgivings about her work place, Kayla had talked to about her idea. Okay, the second, but Dylan didn't count, especially after his less than stellar reaction. "You need to wear a bell or something."

"Where would the fun be in that?" Missy teased. Her whiskey brown eyes smiled out from behind square-framed glasses and her full lips were spread in a welcoming smile. "Besides, I have to be sneaky. I never know when someone might be trying to stick a magazine or toy down their pants."

The thought alone was enough to make Kayla feel queasy. "Do you actually try to get it back?"

"Hell no. They don't pay me enough for that."

Kayla doubted the owners paid Missy enough to deal with any of the drama and midnight jerkers that came to the store. Normally, Kayla didn't consider herself the type of person to pass judgment on anyone. She *was* trying to perfect an anal vibrator, so it wasn't as if she had much moral ground to stand on, but still, she did wish her friend worked in a more wholesome environment.

In many ways, Kayla's fear had a lot more to do with Missy's girl-next-door appeal than the actual shop itself. Cute in a studious way, Missy had long chestnut brown hair she kept pinned up all the time. Smaller in height than Kayla, Missy was a full-figured girl and she tried to play down her lush figure with large clothes and a hideous posture that she used to hide her large breasts. It didn't help though, because anyone could tell that beneath her Holly Hobbie persona, Missy was a heartbreaker waiting to come out of her shell.

Besides, Kayla knew men. And nothing worked more for them than the lady in the boardroom/whore in the bedroom façade.

After giving her a quick hug, Missy gestured to her notebook and asked, "How's the planning going?"

"Slow but steady." Kayla had managed, in between sessions of unbelievable love making, to sketch out a few more prototypes. Sketching was as far as it was going to go though if she didn't find any willing test subjects.

"That doesn't sound promising."

"Genius only takes you so far." It was what it was,

and there was no use complaining about something she had no control over. "Besides you know what they say. When life gives you lemons..."

"You make anal vibrators?"

Kayla smiled. "Something like that."

"I take it from your cheery demeanor you haven't found any volunteers?"

"Not a one." Kayla sighed. No matter how hard she tried to stay positive, reality reared its ugly little head. "I was thinking of taking out an ad in the paper."

"Well, before you do that, let me ask around at school. There are lots of desperate, money-hungry college students who could use some extra cash. Straight and gay."

"Really? I didn't even think of that. Missy, you're a life saver." For such a smart girl, Kayla could be extremely stupid sometimes. Approaching college students had never entered her mind. There were no hornier or cash-desperate people on earth. Hell, even Kayla had volunteered a time or two to be a test subject for extra money when she had been in school. The study hadn't helped her insomnia, but it had more than helped her food, or lack thereof, situation

Excited beyond belief, Kayla pulled the smiling girl back into her arms and hugged her as she jumped up and down.

Laughing at Kayla's enthusiasm, Missy pulled back. "I said I'd ask. I can't promise anything."

Kayla was too happy to worry about semantics. Even

if Missy didn't know anyone personally who might be willing to test her toy, Kayla now had a viable group to look into. "If you can, you can. If not, I'll pass out flyers or something myself."

Her comment only seemed to make Missy smile more. "I just bet you would, but before you go traumatizing anyone, let me ask a few of my more adventurous friends if they might be interested."

"That sounds great."

"The only thing is, Kay, I think you're going to have to keep their identities a secret."

She nodded her head in agreement. Kayla didn't care what she had to do to get her test subjects. "No problem."

The dinging of the bell heralded a customer entering and turned Missy's attention towards the front of the store. The man who entered quickly made eye contact before disappearing down the aisle towards the video booths in the back.

Missy shook her head in amusement. "And to think, I thought today was going to be a quiet one."

"Some people start their day out at MacDonald's..."

"And others start their day out here. Lucky me."

"The real question is, do they normally scurry that fast?"

"You have no idea. It's like they're ashamed to be here, but still they come. I just don't get it."

Even Kayla, the queen of oblivion, had to admit the first time she'd come to Harris's she'd been embarrassed.

"Maybe it's not so much that they're ashamed to be here, as it is that they're ashamed to *have* to be."

"I don't think they should be bothered either way. Sex is perfectly natural."

Kayla held her hands up in defense. "I couldn't agree more. That's why I'm trying to cash in on the market. Speaking of cashing, I didn't only come here for research today. I came to buy a few things."

"For your project?"

"No." Kayla smiled wickedly. "For a friend."

Missy crossed her arms over her chest and raised a brow inquisitively. "This sounds like a very lucky friend."

Not only was he lucky, he was about to get lucky as well. "You have no idea."

"Were you looking for something in particular?"

"Something that will knock his socks off."

Missy nodded her head. "I think I have just what you need."

Chapter Six

Two hours after entering his office, Dylan sat in the most boring meeting of his life. It was an important meeting, but dull nevertheless. He and Chris were trying to woo a client, and Chris was giving their usual spiel while Dylan pretended to listen and take notes.

The Anderson brothers owned the local amusement park and it would be a big coup for Dylan and Chris to snag them as clients. This was the final meeting in a series of meetings showing the Andersons just what they could do for their business. As Chris moved to the computer, there was a loud buzz from the intercom. Eliza's voice came over the speaker.

"You have a call on line two, Mr. Thompson," she said with amusement.

Chris shot him a scolding look as he clicked open the PowerPoint presentation and began the slide show. Even Mrs. Howard, who was taking notes, seemed more put out than usual.

"Take a message, please." Smiling apologetically at the two men sitting across from him, Dylan tried to refocus on the meeting at hand.

"It's very important sir. It's Ms. Martin, from Martin Enterprises."

Martin Enterprises? Dylan scrunched his brow together as he tried to place the name. Martin. Martin. Martin. The only Martin he knew...wait. It couldn't be.

Aware that all eyes were focused on him, Dylan tried not to smile as he reached for the phone. "This will only take a moment. I'm sorry. Please continue, Chris."

Turning his back away from a glaring Chris, Dylan pressed line two and put the phone to his ear.

"Hello, Ms. Martin. How can I help you today?"

"I have a big problem that needs your immediate attention," Kayla said softy into the phone.

"Yes, what can I do for you?"

"You can talk to me as I fuck myself with my vibrator."

At her words, all the blood rushed out of Dylan's head and straight to his hardening cock, which had leapt to life inside his pants. Oh, my God. She had to be kidding.

"Could I possibly call you back?" Looking down at his watch frantically, he quickly estimated how much longer he'd be stuck in the meeting. "In, let's say, an hour?"

"No," she said breathlessly into the phone. "I'll be done way before then. Don't you want to help me come?"

This is so not the time for this, Dylan thought as he shifted in his chair, yet he couldn't tell her no. This was like a fantasy come to life. Kayla was managing to turn an ordinary meeting into the erotic dream of a lifetime.

"Well, let me transfer this call to my office and..."

"No, I want you to stay right where you are."

"But, Ms. Martin, I'm in the middle of a meeting."

"And I'm in the middle of sliding this vibrator all around my clit."

Gulping, Dylan tried to still his racing heartbeat. He wasn't sure if he was in heaven or hell.

Breathe, damn it! Breathe!

"Ms. Martin, I know this is important to you, but I—"

"And I'm all wet thinking of you." Kayla interrupted. "Can I have five minutes of your time? You just need to answer yes or no."

Hell, she could have all the time in the world.

Placing his hand over the mouthpiece, Dylan turned around and addressed the Andersons. "This will only take a moment, sorry."

Dylan shot Chris a pleading look for understanding before turning back around and placing the phone to his ear. Just as the receiver hit his ear, he heard Kayla moaning. His cock tightened painfully in his pants, and he ached to reach in and rub it. Dylan felt the pre-cum slip out the head of his cock, as he thought about the risk he was about to take to fulfill this fantasy.

"Yes," he said firmly. "How can I be of assistance?"

"You can help me decide how I want to do this."

"Okay."

"I've just lubed up my anal plug."

"The one you've been modifying?" Dylan asked.

"No, the one I bought today...along with a few accessories."

Bought today? What in the world had his little Professor been up to this morning? "Accessories?"

"Yes, like my egg and some heating oil."

Dylan had no idea what an egg was, but the erotic image going on in his head made his body shudder. The thought of Kayla spread out on her bed with toys placed all around her, her small hand rubbing lubricant up and down the plug before placing it into her rectum, forced Dylan to push himself closer to the table so that he could hide his ever-hardening bulge

"I think you should go with the unmodified version."

"You want me to put the plug in?"

"Yes." Dylan gripped the phone tighter. On second thought, he wanted to put the plug inside of her hot little ass but that wasn't exactly an option right now.

"Okay," she said. "I'm lying on my back, with my legs bent and my feet on the bed."

"Uh huh."

"I'm placing the plug at my hole and," hissing, Kayla's voice broke before continuing, "pushing it in slowly. God..."

"Did you do it?" he demanded urgently. Looking over his shoulder, he lowered his voice and tried to cover his excitement. This was like every adolescent wet dream he had ever had. A sexy woman masturbating while he listened in. The only thing that made this better was she was his sexy woman. His sexy woman who was going to get her ass spanked when he got home.

"Yes," she moaned, "it's in all the way."

"And how is it working for you?"

"It's full...so full, baby."

Not as full as his cock would have her stretched when he had it buried deep inside her ass. "I think the idea you had earlier sounds good to me."

"You mean the vibrator?"

"Yes, that."

"Do you want me to rub it on my clit?"

"Yes, I think that sounds great."

"Me too..." she gasped, as he heard a distant vibrating noise in the background.

He lowered his hand discreetly down into his lap and squeezed his cock. Dylan could feel a small damp spot on the front of his pants from all the pre-cum he was leaking, but short of taking out his cock and jerking off, there was nothing he could do about it. He was going to have to make sure he took his shirt out of his pants as soon as the meeting was over to cover up the stain. But that would have to come later, when he could actually control his breathing again.

Dylan's heart was racing and his mind was in an uproar from the naughty game they were playing. His hand trembled around the phone as he listened to Kayla moaning and chanting his name as she pleasured herself. God, he was going to come any second himself. He needed to think of something else for just a few moments, before he embarrassed himself in front of everyone in the room.

"I'm getting there, baby," she whimpered into the phone. "I'm so close, I'm so close."

"Now put it in," he whispered softly into the phone, and clutched himself tightly as he heard her scream out in ecstasy.

"Oh God! Oh God, Dylan..."

"I'm here." He shuddered as she screamed his name. The need to jerk off was so intense he had to force himself to release his cock. He knew with a complete certainty that if he continued to grip his cock, even slightly, he would come.

Hell, he was almost coming just listening to her get off. His body tingled and his cock begged to be touched, but he rode it out as he listened to her come down from her orgasm.

The way Kayla panted softly in his ear and whimpered his name made Dylan want more than anything to whisper words of endearments to her. To hold her as she shook in the aftermath, and to pet her pussy as she slid the vibrator in and out of her. He needed to get out of here.

"So is everything good now?" Dylan lowered his voice, so he wouldn't disturb her high.

Kayla chuckled softly. "Better than good. Thank you. I couldn't have done it without you."

"No problem."

"I guess our little meeting is up."

Something was up all right, and it damn sure wasn't little. "Yes, Ms. Martin."

"I'll see you later tonight."

"Sooner, I'm thinking." Dylan said, getting himself back under control. His cock was still throbbing but his desire to erupt had diminished greatly.

"Really?"

"Yes. Also I think the unmodified version should stay right where it is."

Silence greeted him and for a moment Dylan wondered if they had been disconnected, but then Kayla spoke hesitantly. "You want me to leave the butt plug in?"

"Yes." She wasn't the only one who could play games. Dylan glanced back down at his watch before speaking again. "Let's say we meet in two hours and discuss it."

"You want me to leave it in for two hours?"

The shock in her voice was nothing compared to what he'd just experienced. If Kayla thought he was going to let her get away with her naughty little stunt, she had another think coming. Not only did Dylan expect to her mind him, he demanded it. "I think you'd be wise to."

"Uh oh." She giggled. "It sounds like I'm in trouble."

"Yes, ma'am," he said with a smile. "So I'll see you in two hours, and I'm serious about my suggestion, Ms. Martin. I think you should comply."

"I will."

"All right then, goodbye."

Dylan hung up the phone feeling better than he had in hours. Little Ms. Kayla thought she was running things, but she was in for a rude awakening. Turning back to the meeting, Dylan addressed the Andersons. "Sorry about that. I had to, umm, instruct a client on the right moves she should make."

Nodding, they turned their attention back to Chris, who continued with his presentation. Dylan adjusted himself again and thought of all the ways he was planning on making Kayla pay.

Kayla eased back on the couch carefully. It was a little harder walking around with a butt plug in than she had originally thought it would be. With the research she had been doing on the Walnut Wand, she had thought it had sounded quite sexy. And for masturbation play like this morning, it was, but for just walking around, it was a tad uncomfortable.

She felt like she was walking around with the world's biggest wedgie. Or a thong on two sizes too small. It did cause a funny sensation, but the majority of the feeling was discomfort. Sighing, she shifted the pillow behind her back and glanced at the clock on the television.

Dylan should be there soon. Just the thought of seeing him excited her. He seemed to really like the phone call this morning, although she probably should have called back once Eliza had told her he was in an important meeting. But the notion of rattling his oh-so-tidy cage was a challenge she couldn't let slip through her fingers.

Kayla would never have imagined phone sex could be so freaking hot. Just listening to him pretend to be all cool and calm when she knew for a fact he was hot and bothered was a turn-on in itself.

Then again almost everything about him was a turn-on. This weekend, especially, had taught her several things about Dylan she never knew before.

Dylan loved being in control and he was a complete auditory-type person. He not only loved to hear her moan, he demanded it. He wouldn't quit until she clawed him and screamed his name, and damn, that man had a talented tongue. Not just for oral pleasure, but he said things that would make a sailor blush.

Making love to him was the most exciting thing she'd ever done in her entire life. Not only because he was damn good at it, but also because making love with someone you trusted, not only with your body but also with your heart, was almost too much to bear.

The trust they had built up in their friendship over the years had enabled them to be more carefree in the bedroom. Just from conversations they'd had over the years, Kayla knew things he liked and didn't like. She wasn't as self-conscious about being nude in front of him as she would have been with a guy she had just met. Mainly because she'd known for years he thought she was attractive and little things, like her not being a size seven, weren't a big deal to him.

Dylan liked her as she was, and for that reason alone, Kayla loved him.

The doorknob turned, dragging Kayla from her thoughts. The sound of the door opening was more arousing than leaving the anal plug in had been. She knew who was coming through her door and what was going to happen when he did.

When Dylan entered the room and shut the door firmly behind him, locking the handle as he closed it, Kayla's stomach tightened with anticipation. She wasn't as naïve as he thought. Kayla knew exactly what she'd be getting herself into when she called him at work.

Loosening his tie, Dylan untied it but left it dangling off his neck as he walked towards her with an intense look in his eyes. A look which promised retribution and pleasure at every turn. Kayla's mouth went dry and it seemed as if all the moisture that had been in her mouth was now gathering in the center of her thighs.

She was going to get punished. And she couldn't wait.

Standing up carefully, Kayla made her way over to him on trembling legs. The dress she'd pulled over her nude body was thin and light. The soft cotton material brushed across her tingling nipples, causing them to harden as the dress swayed around her body.

"Do you still have it in?" he questioned, as he stood in front of her. Taking her in his arms, he gathered her close and pressed her into his hard front. His voice was as firm as the erection held back by his pants.

Nodding her head yes, Kayla was awestruck at the domineering person who stood before her. It was like the Dylan she normally knew was gone, replaced by this stranger, this angry, aroused stranger.

"Good."

Dylan gripped the dress in his hand and pulled it up until she was exposed from the back down. He ran his fingers down her buttocks, cupping her full pale cheeks in his hands. The possessive grip of his touch almost had Kayla melting at his feet. Running his fingers up her crack, he took a cheek in each hand and gently pulled them apart.

Kayla knew without being told what he was doing. Dylan wasn't going to take her word for it. Her face flamed hot as his fingers explored down her seam until they landed on the base of the plug.

Dylan groaned and buried his face in her hair. "Fuck, baby."

He took the words right of her mouth. Kayla moved in and wrapped her arms around him, needing the security of his arms to hold her up. She felt as if she was going to explode. Not from pleasure but from nervous anticipation. Kayla wanted everything his tone and demeanor promised. She wanted him to take her, like only he could.

Kayla took a deep breath in, trying to calm her pounding heart. The smell of her arousal filled her lungs. She was so fucking turned on, and the strange thing was, he hadn't done a single thing to her yet. Just the hint of what was to come had her revving to go.

Dylan tightened his hold on her, bringing her firmly against him. Thanks to him raising her dress up, her bare front was now pressed against his crisp pants. His buckle, cold and hard against her stomach, made her shiver. Not only from the feel of it, but from the thought of what he might do with it.

Kayla's heartbeat increased as he stroked her ass and she gasped as he pulled back his hand and spanked her exposed rear. The shock of what he did smarted more than the actually blow did.

Too surprised to think, Kayla pushed farther into him as he raised his hand and delivered the same stunning blow to her other cheek. Pushing her away from him, he looked down into her upturned face.

"So you want to play games?" he uttered harshly.

God yes! "I thought that was what you wanted."

"You were right, baby. It's exactly what I want." Turning her around, Dylan moved her forward until she was facing a chair, and pulled her dress over her head. Everything happened so fast Kayla hardly had time to react. All she could do was grip the cushioned arm of the chair and hold on for dear life as he positioned her so her ass was exposed to his view. "Now I'm going to give you what you wanted."

A sharp smack forced her forward on the chair. Reaching over the pillowed back to steady herself, Kayla raised up on her tiptoes as he delivered another blow to her tender ass. Her new position exposed not only her ass but her throbbing pussy to his view as well.

And if that wasn't enough to stir her juices, the plug seemed to lodge itself further inside her with every smack of his hand. Kayla couldn't control her moans of delight as he reddened her bottom. It was more than she'd ever imagined it would be and twice as pleasurable.

"Spread your legs," Dylan demanded, as he alternated between one cheek and the other.

Kayla rushed to obey, but still, he didn't let up. Dylan didn't vary his strokes or his speed, allowing her no time to gather herself between blows. Instead, he continued in his course of action. His spanking keeping her on edge with every blow.

Just when Kayla thought she couldn't stand a second more of the sensual torture, a sharp slap landed between her thighs, lightly stinging her clitoris before returning to her cheeks. At first, she thought it might have been an accident, but then Dylan did it again and again. The heated sensation caused her to bite down on her lip to keep from screaming out in pleasure. Her pussy was on fire, partly from the blows and partly from the spanking in general.

"Dylan..." She moaned, unable to stop the sob from escaping. Kayla was a hair's breadth away from coming, and all he had done was spank her.

Her outcry stilled his hand and much to her surprise, Dylan dropped to his knees behind her. Leaning forward slowly, he placed gentle kisses on her sensitive reddened cheeks.

The sweet sensation on her tender backside made

Kayla's heart skip a beat. He was so forceful yet so gentle all at the same time. Before she could wax poetic about his virtues, she felt his wet tongue trail across her burning backside.

Lifting her ass higher, she slipped her hand down between the chair and her sopping pussy to finger herself. She had always had a secret fantasy about being spanked. When she had asked him to do it during intercourse, she sensed his shock and then his excitement, but nothing had prepared her for today.

To ask a man to spank her during sex was one thing, but to have Dylan sense her desire, no, her need of it today was another thing completely. He was, by far, the most in tune and giving lover she had ever had, almost too good to be true.

Dylan kissed his way across her heated cheek to the plug lodged firmly in her depths. But he didn't stop there. He went down further until he reached the entrance of her wet center. He cleansed the juices from between her thighs before he plunged his tongue into her creamy core, lavishly stroking her mound. Reaching up, he grabbed her hands and stopped her from stroking her clit. He pulled her hand away and then replaced her probing fingers with his own as he slid his tongue into her pussy.

"Ohhh." Kayla dug her fingers into her chair to steady herself as she felt herself near climax.

His fingers played her like a piano. Teasing, taunting, milking her to orgasm as he lapped at her cream like a cat. Moaning, she bit her lip and pressed her back into him as she came, screaming into a throw pillow. It was like no other orgasm she'd ever experienced before. Sure, her body shook and her knees trembled and the gates of heaven opened up. But still there was so much more.

Her skin was so hot Kayla was surprised the chair didn't burst into flames within her grasp. Her body felt too weak to be able to hold her soul in. By the very definition of the word, Kayla felt well and truly fucked.

Dylan pulled back as she tried to get herself together. Pushing up from the chair, she stayed bent slightly forward as she gathered the strength to stand straight up. She wasn't sure if it was from lack of oxygen or from the mind-bending orgasm, but she couldn't seem to get her feet to work.

"Come on." Pulling her away from the chair, Dylan helped her to the floor. "Get up on all fours," he said as she sat down on the floor. Dylan began to get undressed as she positioned herself as he had instructed.

Kayla was amazed at her meekness, but having her ass spanked did kind of bring that out in her. Facing him, she watched as he slid his pants down past his straining cock, and licked her lips in appreciation. She hoped he planned for her to give him head. Nothing tasted better than his hard cock sliding between her lips.

"I don't think so, pretty baby." He chuckled as he watched her lick her lips.

Damn it, the man was a mind reader and a fucking tease.

"I'll be right back." Dylan said, as he headed out of the room. He was only gone for a few seconds, but when he returned, he came bearing gifts.

Dylan held the mirror she had on the back of her door in his hands. Propping it against the couch, he leaned it so that they could see themselves. Kneeling behind her, he positioned them so that they could see a side view of their reflection.

"Oh my..." she muttered, looking at his hungry expression in the mirror. Just the idea of what he was planning had her creaming again. She had never felt this alive, this free with anyone before. Kayla knew right then and there that there wasn't anything that she wouldn't do for him, or to him.

Chapter Seven

As if entranced by her ruby flesh, Dylan sat back and stared at his handiwork. Her rear was lit with red handprints, bright and varied on her plump cheeks. A sense of pride filled him as he looked at his woman marked with his brand. Never before had he felt this Neanderthal with a woman, but for some reason Kayla brought out the caveman in him.

He wanted the world to know she belonged to him. But more importantly, he wanted Kayla to know it. After today, she wouldn't be able to sit, shower, or pass a mirror naked without remembering what took place this afternoon.

To be truthful, Dylan was surprised by the way spanking her had gotten him so hard. Not that he needed any help in that department. Ever since their little phone call, Dylan's cock had been primed to go. Yet the moment he lit into her backside, he went from aroused to ready to burst.

It had taken everything inside him not to plunge into her right away. But now, the waiting was over. Rubbing his hand down the length of his erect cock, Dylan looked over into the mirror. The sight of her watching back caused his cock, if it was possible, to harden further.

Spreading her lips apart, he slid into her hot channel, gasping at the pleasure of seeing and feeling her all at the same time. Pulling back, he tunneled into her as he rubbed her reddened ass and watched as she pumped back into him. They were both watching the show, a show more arousing than any porn he had ever seen. The fact that she could see him and what he was doing to her was beyond sexy in his opinion.

Breaking eye contact with the scene in the mirror, Dylan looked down at her ass, which still contained the plug. Reaching down, he grabbed the base of the plug and slid it slowly out of her tight hole. Careful not to bring it all the way out, he twisted it inside of her and pushed it quickly back in, causing her to shove back into him and cry out in pleasure.

Twisting and turning the plug as he fucked her, Dylan quickly brought Kayla back to the edge. It didn't take much to get his little fuck baby there. She seemed always eager for his touch. Her moans escalated as she shoved back onto his thick member.

"That's it, baby," he groaned between clenched teeth. Dylan had never felt anything so incredible in his life. He could feel the plug as he fucked her. It was a heavy sensation pressing against his penis, only separated by a thin layer of tissue. It caused pressure on the top of his cock and it felt wonderful. He wondered what a vibrator would feel like buried in her ass and if he would be able to feel it vibrating against him as well. Just the thought had him clenching his teeth, holding back the orgasm threatening to spill from him.

"Dylan... I can't, I'm so close," she moaned as she slipped her hand beneath her torso and fingered her clit.

Dylan watched in the mirror as Kayla rubbed her clit faster. The sight of her masturbating was more than he could bear. He pushed into her again, feeling her tighten around him. Kayla gushed his name as she arched her back and came, screaming "fuck me" at the top of her lungs.

Dropping down on her elbows, Kayla lowered her breasts onto the plush carpet, enabling Dylan to fuck her deeper. He pumped his cock into her, gripping her hips in his strong hands he pulled her body into his as he ground against her, coming into her moist channel.

"Fuck." Dylan's body shook with his release. Kayla just whimpered as he slowly began to slide his still-hard cock in and out of her, as if trying to milk every last drop out of his engorged flesh.

Sweat ran down Dylan's back and pooled at his hips. Reaching between her flushed cheeks Dylan gently pulled the plug out as she sighed in relief. Slowly pulling out of her gripping body, he sat back on his heels and labored to catch his breath. Kayla crawled forward until her entire body was flat on the floor and whimpered when she rolled over and one of her tingling cheeks made contact with the carpet.

Tossing the plug to the side, Dylan reached over to the end table, picked up a tissue and wiped his moist cock before tossing the tissue over his shoulder and joining Kayla on the carpet. Spooning her, he lay for a moment, just breathing in the scent of their sex, enjoying the spicy aroma of their loving as it lingered in the air. He pulled her in deep to him and placed his hands between her rising breasts, over her heart.

He had never felt so completely drained in his life. This little fireball had managed, in one day, to fulfill several pubescent fantasies and still leave him wanting more. The fact that she trusted him enough to allow him to spank her was such an honor. An overwhelming feeling, a sense of pride filled his ever-growing ego. She was good for his libido, in more ways than one.

Kayla reached up, entwined her fingers with his over her heart and squeezed his hand.

"They should write folk songs about you."

"You say that as if they don't," he joked.

Kayla let out a soft chuckle, which made his heart tighten even more inside his exhausted body. Leaning over, he released her fingers and brought his hand up and under her chin. Dylan gently nudged her face up towards his as he lowered his lips and took her mouth in a tender kiss.

His lips lightly grazed hers before she opened her mouth and lapped at his tongue with hers. Dylan deepened the kiss, savoring her sweet taste, familiar, distinctive and so uniquely hers. A taste he had come to need like air.

Pulling away from her, he stared into her upturned

face and smiled. She was more beautiful at this moment, flushed and exhausted from their loving, than she had ever been before. He loved seeing that look on her face. It brought out the caveman in him, to know he had such an effect on her. The same effect she unknowingly had on him.

"I didn't hurt you, did I?" he asked.

"Did I sound like I was hurting?"

"I don't know. It all depends on how you translate, 'fuck me, baby, fuck me', but I guess it could go either way."

Laughing softly, she rolled over until she was facing him, wincing a little as her tender hide brushed against the carpet. When he frowned, Kayla quickly replaced her look of pain with a look of tenderness.

Dylan had slightly flinched when she winced. He knew he was a strong guy, he just hoped he hadn't accidentally hurt her.

"I'm fine, papa bear." Kayla ran her hand lovingly across his cheek, leaned up and cupped his jaw. "But next time I get to be the boss of you."

Groaning, Dylan rolled onto his back, pulling Kayla up more on her side, so that she was lying half on him and half on the floor.

"I don't think I could handle you."

"Damn straight you couldn't." Laughing softly, they drifted into comfortable silence.

Dylan gently stroked her back as Kayla faintly ran her

fingers across his chest. Her gentle touch comforted him in a small way. This was the part of lovemaking he had never allowed before, the intimate part, but with Kayla not only did he allow it, he craved it.

"Did you enjoy your phone call today?" Kayla asked, breaking the silence.

"More than words could say."

"Good," she said, with a smile in her tone. "Just wait until you see what I have in store for you tomorrow."

"When you said wait to see what I have planned for you tomorrow, I was thinking something a bit less...sleazy," Dylan grumbled, as he stood outside of Harris's.

"There's nothing sleazy about this place," Kayla said, ringing the doorbell. "An old client of mine works here and this place will be perfect for research."

"What are you going to do, approach different men and ask them if they like their walnut being manipulated?" Seeing the thoughtful look on her face, he quickly added, "That was a joke, Kayla."

"A good idea is a good idea," she mumbled, as the buzzer sounded and the door opened. They walked through the doors and down the aisle lined with shelves of movies.

Kayla waved at Missy who was working at the counter as usual. Missy quickly raised her hand and waved back, smiling all the while.

"And it's not like I dragged you here, you know. You didn't have to come."

"Like I'm going to let to you come to a place like this at eleven at night."

Kayla was willing to bet Dylan wouldn't have let her come to "a place like this" no matter what the time was. For that reason alone, she was going to keep to herself how often she made trips here. She might be flaky, but she wasn't dumb. "Then shut your pie hole and go grab an anal plug."

Chuckling to herself, Kayla laughed at the flicker of surprise that flashed across his face. Walking around the corner, she took out her small notebook and pen from her back pocket. She really had come to do some research and also to talk to Missy about the new recruits.

Kayla had made the unfortunate mistake of mentioning to Dylan she was coming tonight, and he had insisted on getting out of bed to come with her. Not that she wouldn't enjoy the company, but she did have to listen to him complain the whole ride over.

"I'm not going anywhere near any butt plugs," commented Dylan, as he stopped in front of the vibrator displays.

Snorting, Kayla eyed him amusedly. "So you have absolutely no problem using one on me, but you refuse to go to the section where they are."

"Lower your voice," he whispered, glancing around. "It's one thing to use one on you, it's another thing to hang out in the butt plug section while you take notes. And what happens if I run into a client here?"

"Dylan." The exasperation in her voice was mixed with amusement. He was so clueless at times. "I guarantee if you see a client in here, he'll be just as embarrassed as you and probably run the other way."

Noticing the stubborn look on his face, Kayla sighed and gave into him. Pointing in the opposite direction, she sarcastically said, "Why don't you go stand over there next to the cards and stuff? You'll be able to keep an eye on me in case any bad pervert comes over and asks if he can plug me."

Narrowing his eyes, Dylan grunted and crossly walked the few feet away, turned and faced her, crossing his arms on his chest. *He is really something else*, thought Kayla amusedly as she turned and walked over to the anal toy section.

There are so many toys on the market, she thought, tapping her pen against her leg.

Big plugs, small plugs, even plugs that glowed in the dark. Kayla picked up a cone-shaped, neon pink one that was the size of a large, squeezable mustard bottle and automatically clenched her butt cheeks. This one had a bullet that went inside of it, causing it to vibrate, close to what she was thinking of for The Walnut Wand, but shaped completely differently.

She was thinking of something similar to a vibrator combined with a butt plug, but geared towards men. Kayla wasn't sure of the dimensions yet, but she'd gotten all the wiring and mechanical stuff almost worked out. Deep in thought, she jumped when someone touched her arm. Swinging around, she breathed a sigh of relief when she recognized Missy.

"You have got to stop scaring me."

"You know," Missy smiled, "if you were living right, you wouldn't be so damn jumpy."

"Tell me something I don't know."

"Purple tie-dyed shirts with green stretch paints don't match."

Kayla burst out laughing as she looked down at her outfit. Okay, so it wasn't very Vogue, but it was comfortable as hell. "Touché, my friend."

"What are you doing out so late?"

"I had a new idea and I came here to brainstorm." Gesturing over to a scowling Dylan, she continued, "Although if I didn't have to bring my watchdog, things would be going a heck of a lot quicker."

Looking to where Kayla pointed, Missy gave a low whistle and whispered under her breath. "You're complaining about that guy? He can eat cookies in my bed anytime."

"Sweetie, if he's in your bed, I would suggest that you give him something besides cookies to eat," teased Kayla.

Missy burst out laughing, causing her entire face to glow. "You're terrible."

Kayla grinned proudly. "I know."

"It's a good thing you stopped by."

"Really, why?"

"Because I spoke with a few guys at school today and I think I might have found you a few test subjects."

"Shut up!" Kayla squealed as she grabbed Missy's hands. "Are you serious?"

Laughing, Missy shook her head as Kayla bounced up and down. "Completely."

"Missy..." Kayla couldn't even finish her sentence let alone her thought. She wanted to scream. She wanted to shout. She wanted to jump for joy. "I can't thank you enough."

"You can start by releasing my hands."

"Oh." Poor girl. In her excitement Kayla had damn near broke her fingers. "Sorry."

"No problem. I'll email you their phone numbers tonight."

"That would be wonderful." Kayla couldn't wait to tell Dylan. Whirling around, she looked for him, but was brought up short by very uncomfortable look on his face. "Doesn't he just look miserable?"

Glancing over her shoulder at Dylan, Missy nodded her agreement. Dylan was trying to blend in with other browsing customers by flipping through the cards but it was very obvious that he was out of his element.

Kayla got an idea. Pulling Missy in closer, she whispered to her, "Have the movie booths been really busy tonight?"

"Not especially."

"Do you think you can overlook it if we slip into one? I know it's only supposed to be one person per booth, but..."

Raising her hand to silence her, Missy's hazel eyes twinkled from behind her glasses. "Say no more. I have a very simple rule when it comes to the booths. What happens in there, stays in there."

Kayla smiled and whispered her thanks. Walking over to Dylan, she lightly touched him on the shoulder, causing him to jump.

"You done already?" he asked excitedly.

"No, I need to go check out a movie."

"Check it out, as in the library?"

"No." She chuckled, pointing past the sex toys to a door that led to a hall. "We have to go around the corner and they have some booths, where you can check out part of a movie."

There were four doors against the wall in the hall. Each door had a token box, a movie folder and an electriconic keypad. Kayla sent Dylan over to the change machine and had him exchange some ones for some tokens. Flipping through the folder, Kayla picked out the code of the movie she wanted to see, deposited her token and pulled an unwilling Dylan into the doorway of the booth.

The small booth was the size of a photo booth like the ones on the piers. It would be a tight fit, but Kayla knew any second of discomfort would soon be forgotten. A small retractable bench faced a mini television screen installed into the wall. Glancing around, she contemplated how the two of them were going to do this before finally deciding they were just going to have to stand up.

"This place is a little dingy." Keeping his hand in his pocket, Dylan looked around the box distastefully. "You know what people do in here, don't you?"

"I know what we're going to do in here," she said, smiling as she shut the door.

Dropping her notebook on the bench, Kayla turned so she was standing in front of him with her back pressed into his chest. They moved back away from the screen, placing as much distance between themselves and the TV monitor.

The room immediately went dark and the television screen lit up. The film popped on mid-movie, showing a woman being pounded doggie-style by one man while she gave head to another.

Dylan stopped his grumbling almost instantaneously and focused on the movie playing. Leaning back into him, Kayla slid her hand behind her and laid it on the zipper of his pants.

"Kayla," warned Dylan, looking down at her.

Kayla smiled up at him and whispered, "Watch the film," as she began to manipulate his penis through his jeans.

Squeezing gently, she felt it beginning to stir, rising slowly as she pressed her fingers around the outline in the denim.

Turning around, she faced him and unbuttoned and

unzipped his pants. Kayla got up on her tiptoes so she was able to slide her hand around his neck and bring him down for a kiss. Drinking in his sweet taste, Kayla's lips caressed his before she dipped her tongue between his parted lips. Their tongues intertwined, slipping and sliding against one another. Playful, she pulled back and gently captured his bottom lip between her teeth, nipping at it.

Growling, Dylan pulled her back into him, taking command of her mouth. His hand tangled with her soft hair and he made love to her mouth as the sounds of passion from the movie echoed all around them. Kayla ran her hands down his shoulder to the front of his pants. Pulling them open, she scratched her nails lightly against his tense abdomen.

Pulling gently but firmly on her hair, Dylan drew her mouth from his, and hissed. "There isn't room in here for this. Let's take this somewhere more private."

"There's plenty of room in here for what I have mind." She smiled.

Moving her hand lower, Kayla wrapped her fingers around his stiffening cock.

Pumping him, she stroked him to full mast as she listened to the sound of the movie in the background. Kayla tingled from head to toe and her stomach clenched with desire. She wasn't sure if it was because of the actors and their moans or the fact she was giving him a hand job in the middle of a semi-crowded store. Whatever it was, it was causing her to soak her panties in excitement.

Kayla caressed him, moving her hand slowly up and down his thick erection. She loved the sensation of him in her hand, so hard and alive. The feel of him growing harder and longer, his flesh hot and thick, pulsating between her fingers, urging her on, was the biggest power trip for her in the world. Dropping to her knees in front of him, she looked up into his shocked eyes as she licked the head of his cock.

Reaching behind him, she clicked the latch holding the bench down and pushed it up, giving them more legroom. Dylan stepped back as she shimmied his pants down his hips a bit and looked up at him. Excitement shone from his face, his eyes filled with passion and his breath deepened.

"I want you to have the best of both worlds." She gestured with her head to the screen behind her. "You can listen to them moan and fuck up there and you can feel my mouth around you here."

Kayla could tell by his expression he had simply thought she was going to give him a hand job and although he was slightly worried about being caught, she knew he wanted this more by the way his stomach contracted against her hands. Pressing an open-mouthed kiss to his stomach, she licked and bit gently before sliding his hard cock into her mouth.

"Kayla, if I have to call Chris to bail us out, I'm going to kill you," he whispered softly.

Pulling his erection out of her mouth, she smiled and brought her finger up to her lips to shush him. Taking him back in her mouth, she bathed his crown with her tongue, enjoying the smooth feel of him and his mild flavor. Pre-cum trickled from his slit and she lapped it up, drinking in his salty taste. Wrapping her teeth around the crown, she lightly grazed him before taking his length into her mouth.

Kayla smiled around his cock when she heard a groan come from Dylan and pushed all of him into her mouth until the head just reached the back of her throat. Pulling it out, she encircled the top, milking the tip before sliding it back in. She ran her hand up his cock, stroking and sucking him at the same time. Looking up she saw the look of rapture shining in his face as she deep-throated his thick member.

Reaching out, Dylan placed his hands on the walls of the booth, steadying himself as she worked his cock. Kayla watched as she sucked him and enjoyed seeing him fight for control. Taking his balls into her hands, she massaged them as she quickened her motions with her mouth.

"Fuck..." he muttered, as his balls tightened and he came, pouring into her mouth.

Swallowing, Kayla gently pumped his cock until she thought he was through.

Pulling slowly away, she stroked him softly, licking the crown, cleaning all traces of his semen from him. Blowing softly, she chuckled as he hissed at her and took his cock from her hands, stuffing it back in his pants.

Standing, Kayla leaned forward and kissed him.

Dylan pulled her in tighter and devoured her mouth. Her tongue caressed his, moving back and forth, deeper and harder, until they had to pull back to breathe.

Leaning forward, he rested his forehead against hers and stared into her eyes. "You are certifiable."

Laughing, she quickly pressed her lips against his for a quick kiss. "And you love it."

"Every fucking second of it." Dylan quickly buttoned and zipped up his pants. As if in a hurry, he reached behind him and pulled the stool down.

"Are we in rush to get out of here?"

"Yes, we are." Dylan grabbed her notebook and shoved it in her hands. "I hope you know we're going straight home."

"What about my research?" Kayla asked, amused.

"I plan on giving you all the research material you'll need."

Whether Dylan meant it as a threat or a promise, it didn't really matter to her. The way he said it flat out worked for Kayla. Sliding back the door, she peeked around the sides, checking to see if the coast was clear. Pulling him quickly from the closet-sized booth, they hustled out the door.

As they walked past the counter, Kayla smiled at a grinning Missy, who winked at Dylan, causing him to blush and walk faster out the door.

"Ya'll come back now, you hear," Missy called out quickly before the door shut, cutting off her laughter.

Chapter Eight

The sound of the door being slammed shut echoed through the apartment. The familiar noise brought a quick smile to Dylan's face. He and Kayla both had been working a lot in the last week, making it very difficult for them to find time to be together.

Strangely, Dylan had found himself not only missing the sex between him and the Professor, but her company as well. This was the first time all week that the sound of her bare feet slapping against the wooden floor had rung out and he missed it, almost as much as he missed her.

"Morning," he called out, as he closed his bedroom closet, but when he turned around what he saw startled him. His Energizer Bunny looked, for the lack of a better word, run down.

Kayla was dressed in her normal bright, badly put together outfit, but it was the lackluster look on her face that held his attention. Dark shadows circled her eyes and her skin was missing its usual glow. The sign of strain was evident in her face, breaking Dylan's heart in half.

"Rough night?"

"In a word." Kayla yawned, stretching her arms high above her head. The mustard yellow shirt she wore rose with her movement, bringing her pale tummy into view. Dylan had to focus hard to keep his gaze from traveling down her body.

This was not the time to think with his cock. It was time to think with his heart.

Dylan walked over to her and pulled his tired cherub into his arms. "When was the last time you slept?"

Kayla snuggled against his chest and loosely wrapped her arms around his waist. "Tenth grade, remember?"

"I'm serious, Kay."

Sighing, Kayla curled into him like a kitten. "It's been a long week."

"Okay, let me rephrase my question." Dylan brushed her dark locks away from her forehead, replacing her bangs with soft kisses. "If you had to estimate, how much sleep do you think you've had this week?"

"All together?"

"Yes."

"I'd say…" Her silence wasn't very reassuring. "Maybe ten or twelve hours."

Dylan closed his eyes in resignation. Even after all this time, one would think he'd be used to her hectic schedule. But used to it or not, it was no way for anyone to live. Kayla was so tired she was practically dead on her feet.

"Don't worry. All I need is a cup of your world famous

coffee and I'll be better than new."

"Coffee is the last thing you need."

Kayla pulled away and looked at him. Her full lips were spread in that secret smile of hers he'd come to love so much. "You think you know what I need better than I do?"

"Think, no. I know I do. You need a keeper."

"Applying for the job?"

"Someone has to. You're going to run yourself into the grave."

"I'm just a little tired."

"A little tired." Dylan resisted the urge to snort his amusement. "That's an understatement. Your bags have bags."

"You're not much on the flattery today."

"You don't need flattery. You need sleep."

Kayla tried to shrug her shoulders as if she didn't care, but the movement made her look more exhausted than she had before. "I'll sleep when I'm dead."

"Which, by the looks of you, will be more like sooner than later." Dylan wasn't kidding. Kayla needed a keeper in the worse way and he was more than man enough for the job. "Come on, Professor, it's time for you to go to bed."

When he reached to take her hand, Kayla pulled away from him. Her resisting him was almost as surprising as her tired appearance. Kayla had never pulled away from him.

"I'm not going to be able to go to sleep."

"I promise you, you will."

Kayla's brows rose. "Really? You think that you can cure what countless doctors and mounds of medication couldn't?"

"I have a secret weapon that none of them did."

"What's that?"

"I know you." There, his secret was out.

"And..."

"And I know that since we've been together, you've been getting a lot more sleep when you're in my bed." Try as he might, Dylan couldn't keep the hint of pride out of his tone. After all these years, he'd finally found away to help Kayla burn some of her energy off.

Sighing, Kayla smiled warily. "Dylan, I'll never be able to sleep here with you gone. Really, it was a nice offer and all, but eventually, I'll get so tired my body will just shut down and I'll get some rest. Trust me, I've been doing this for years."

And look where it got you. The words were on the tip of his tongue but Dylan chewed them back one bloody bite at a time. "Who said anything about me going anywhere?"

"Unless I'm delusional, and trust me, with as little of sleep as I've gotten, the possibility is more than there, today is a Thursday."

"Yes."

"You have to work on Thursday."

"I'm not going to work today."

"But..." Kayla's eyes widened as if she were shocked. "What do you mean you're not going? You always go to work. Even when you're sick. Even on holidays, you go to work."

Her disbelief was proof enough that he worked too much. Not that he needed it. Dylan was more than aware of his work ethic and overdrive, and because of everything Kayla pointed out, he was also aware he had more than enough vouchers to call in so he could take the day off to take care of her.

For once in his life, Dylan was going to put someone—no not just someone—he was going to put Kayla ahead of everything else in his life.

"But...but..."

"Kayla." Amused, Dylan moved until he was once again standing directly in front of her. Her once-tired eyes now beamed up a look of confusion that made him want to laugh. Did she really think he was so incapable of missing work for one little day? This time Dylan wasn't going to let her pull away from him. He gripped her hands in his tightly, making sure not to break eye contact, so that his words were heard loud and clear. "The world will not come to an end because I don't show up today. Chris is more than capable of handling anything that pops up, and even if he isn't, too damn bad. Today, I'm taking care of you."

"It's not necessary."

"It is to me."

"I don't know what to say."

That was a first. His little Chatty Cathy was speechless. Dylan was going to have to mark this day down on the calendar. "I don't suppose you consider saying 'Yes, Master'."

"Uh no." She laughed. "I'm not that tired."

"It was worth a try." Dylan dropped a quick kiss on her upturned brow. "Now hightail yourself into the bathroom and get undressed. I'm going to start you a bath and fix you something soothing to drink."

"Coffee?"

"Warm milk."

"Now you're just being cruel."

"No back talk, woman," he teased, nudging her in the direction of the bathroom. Dylan slapped her on the ass as she passed by him. He was doing a good deed, but he was far from a saint.

Her shout of laughter was soon followed by her not so meek reply of "Yes Master", which in turn brought a smile to his face. Maybe playing hookey wasn't so bad after all.

"Yes, sir, I'll let Chris and Mrs. Howard know." Eliza tried her best to keep her surprise out of her voice. The office atmosphere was casual and all, but somehow she seriously doubted her boss would take to her stuttering "are you sure'" to him.

After writing down his message, Eliza hung up the phone, with a look of wonder on her face. Just when she thought nothing in life could surprise her anymore, something up and did.

In all the time she worked at Thompson and Wilson Financing Company, Dylan Thompson had never called in. Truth be told, Eliza couldn't actually recall if he had taken vacation either. He was the epitome of a workaholic, dedicated and overly obsessed with his career.

Dylan seemed driven to succeed for the sake of success, whereas Chris on the other hand, always seemed as if he were driven to succeed by an unwavering force. Almost as if he had something to prove. There was an underlying force in him, a method to his madness some might say, but for the life of Eliza, she couldn't figure out what it was.

Nor could she figure out what it was about her boss that made her think about him more than she should. The last thing she needed right now was to get involved with a man, let alone her boss. It was only by the grace of God she had this job to begin with. Divorced single moms weren't high on employers' dream lists and what had started out as a temp position had blossomed into a full-time gig.

Office assistant positions for good companies didn't come around every day. Sure the job had its downs, like having to work with the sour puss Mrs. Howard, but it also had its perks as well. A few of which were the great pay, the friendly atmosphere, and her dream man working just a few feet away. Too bad he was her boss.

"Has Dylan come in yet?"

Speaking of her dream man, Eliza looked up and into the deepest, darkest eyes she'd ever seen and tried her best not to drool. The man was drop-dead gorgeous. Almost too pretty for his own, and her own, good. Well over six feet tall, Chris had the body that should grace the covers of fashion magazines.

With skin the color of deep ebony and a muscular physique that even the most expensive tailored suits couldn't hide, Chris was pure sin wrapped up in a yummy package.

"Eliza."

Eliza was so focused on her mental drooling that she continued to stare at him, not answering his summons. "Eliza!"

"Oh. Sorry."

"Where were you?" Chris leaned against her desk and regarded her with an amused look. The dark eyes she had just moments earlier contemplated diving in now were swimming with laughter.

"Uh..." Heat bloomed in her cheeks. "La la land, don't mind me. What did you say?"

"La la land, huh? From the embarrassed look on your face, I'd say 'la la land' is an R-rated place to live." His voice was so warm and deep it made her knees tremble. It was a good thing she was sitting down, because her legs felt weak just being near him.

"You have no idea."

"Don't I?"

Times like these she wished her office were larger, because every time Chris talked to her, he somehow always ended up leaning against her desk. His firm, mouth-watering body just inches away from her fingers. Clearing her throat, Eliza tried to summon forth a professional demeanor. "What can I help you with?"

Chris continued watching her with his panty-dampening stare. It took everything in Eliza to control her urge to squirm under his penetrating gaze. If he didn't watch himself, she was going to give him something to look at all right. Eliza might be treading on the cautious side, but she wasn't a coward.

"Well..." Eliza dragged out the word, hoping to spur him into action, but it was to no avail. He continued to watch her. Fed up, Eliza blurted out the only thing she could think of, "Do you like what you see?"

The words that slipped out surprised not only Eliza, but from the wide eyed look on his face, Chris as well. One moment she was trying not to fidget, and the next she was daring him to make a move.

A slow sexy smiled spread out across his full lips, making Eliza wonder what it would feel like to have those same lips pressed against hers. Or even better, pressed lower down on her body.

"Yes, I do, but that's neither here or there." Apparently, she wasn't the only one who thought their conversation needed to get back on track. "What I originally asked you was if Dylan had come in yet."

"No, he called a few minutes ago, and the call was

transferred to my line."

"Mrs. Howard out?"

"For a moment it seemed, but she's not the only one."

"What do you mean?"

"Dylan isn't coming in today. He said he's taking a personal day."

"A personal day?" The astonished look on Chris's face was priceless. Apparently she wasn't the only person who was shocked by Dylan's no show. "Is he sick?"

"He didn't sound sick."

"Did someone die?"

Eliza laughed at the dumbfounded tone in his voice. Either Dylan was going to have to start taking more time off or figure out a better way to brace Chris when he did. "No, no death. No destruction. No illness. He was just taking a personal day."

"Well, I'll be damned."

"There's nothing on the books today. I'm sure we'll be fine."

"It's not that. Hell, Dylan has more time coming to him than everyone else in the company put together. I'm just surprised. He doesn't...normally call in."

"Has he ever?"

Chris tilted his head to the side and drew his brows together as if in thought. "Not that I can recall."

"Then it's probably long over due."

"I don't disagree. He's like James Brown, the hardest working man in the business."

"I think you work pretty hard yourself."

"I do." Chris smiled. "But I'm not insane about it. I know when to go home and how to have fun."

"Really..." Now that sounded promising.

"Yes." Shaking his head, Chris stood up. "I don't suppose you're going to be the one to break it to Mrs. Howard?"

In his dreams. Eliza wasn't easily intimidated but there was just something about that woman that made her stomach tighten up just like it did in high school when she was sent to the principal's office for ditching. "You don't pay me enough."

Chris laughed. "Say no more."

Just when Chris turned to leave, Eliza remembered the message she had written down for him. "Chris, wait."

"Yes."

Steeling her tepid nerves, Eliza grabbed the note from the desk and handed it to him. Try as she might, Eliza wasn't able to hand off the small paper without brushing her fingers against his. The small contact sent an electric current through her body. If she hadn't been aware of him before, the sensation of touching him brought her awareness to the front and center. She didn't know how much longer she could play this teasing game without some conclusion.

"Here is your message."

Chris didn't even look down at the paper, instead he kept his gaze firmly locked on hers. "Thank you."

The world around them seemed to come to a standstill as they both held on to the paper, fingers lightly touching. Every emotion, every secret longing that Eliza had kept deep inside bubbled forth.

Even though her common sense warned her of the consequence, Eliza knew, whether it was a good idea or not, they were so taking this to the next level.

It was truly only a matter of time.

Chapter Nine

The bed dipping roused Dylan from his deep sleep. Without opening his eyes, he reached behind him and pulled Kayla's chilly arm over his side and tucked her hand against his chest. It was late, hell it had been late when he went to bed. "I guess your vacation is over."

Kayla snuggled up behind him, pressing her nude body to his back. It was hard to stay mad at her or to fall back asleep when she fought back so brilliantly. "If I recall correctly, you went back to work before I did."

"What are you talking about?" Dylan turned his head to peer at her in the dark.

"I saw you check your email this afternoon."

Dylan turned his head so she wouldn't see him smile. She caught that, did she? He had only missed two days of work so far, but still he was already jonesing. He was just as addicted to work as Kayla claimed he was, but that didn't mean he was going to admit it. "I was looking at porn."

"Liar." She laughed, snuggling up closer. "Porn would never be that boring. Just admit it, you can't stay away from work anymore than I can."

"True, but at least I sleep." Dylan wasn't sure how he felt about comparing his work to hers, but neither was he dumb enough to admit it.

Hell, he didn't even want to bring up the Walnut Wand for fear Kayla hadn't gotten it out of her head to use him as a test subject. There were many things he was willing to do for his brown-haired vixen, but sacrificing his anal virginity wasn't one of them.

Kayla tugged her hand free and slowly ran it down his chest to his flat stomach before slipping it beneath the boxers he had pulled on after his shower. Dylan felt his cock stir as she teasingly brushed her fingers against him. "Sleep isn't everything, besides why do you think I'm here?"

"Because you were out of groceries."

"Yes, but also because I need my nightly dose of sleeping semen."

Dylan's laughter rang out in the dark room. "Sleeping semen?"

"Uh huh. I've been told by the supplier it has ingredients in it that I need to knock out my insomnia."

"And do you take it regularly?"

"I plan on it." Dylan bit back a groan as she ran her hand up his rigid length. It was a tight fit, because he still had the boxers on, but it didn't seem to deter Kayla. "From the feel of this, I think you have exactly what I need for my nightly dose. Now there's really only one question left."

"What's that?"

"How should I take it? Orally or anally."

Dylan closed his hand over hers, stopping Kayla from her depraved torture. He wasn't quite sure which was worse, her pumping hand or her dirty words. "You shouldn't tease a man about anal sex."

"Who's teasing?" Kayla leaned over and nipped at his ear. "I've been a very good girl."

"How good?"

"Very."

That's exactly what he wanted to hear. Anal sex to him was never a question of if they were going to do it, only when. Since the day he and Kayla used the plug, Dylan had instructed her to wear it at least two hours a day. He wanted her to be able to take his thick length when the time was right without hesitation or much pain.

In fact, it had actually become a little dominant game between the two of them. He'd call her from work and instruct her to put it in. Speaking in low tones, he would tell her how he wanted her to be positioned when she used it and what he wanted her to do while it was in. He was officially jerking off more now than he ever had as a teenager, and yet it didn't seem to help keep his desire for her at bay.

They were fucking like the cure for cancer was buried deep inside her pussy and he was on a quest to find it. They had even implemented the anal toy into their sex play on a regular basis. Dylan had placed toys, his fingers, even his tongue into the tight recesses of her ass. The only thing left to put there now was his cock. And there was no time better than the present.

Dylan reluctantly pulled Kayla's hand from beneath his boxers and away from his throbbing cock so he could turn around and face her. Even in the dark he could see the mischievous smile lingering on her lips. She was so fucking beautiful, she took his breath away. "Are you wearing it now?"

"Yes."

Dylan looped his hand behind her knee and brought her leg up to rest on his hip as he slipped a thigh between hers. He wanted to find out for himself just how *good* Kayla had been. Taking his time, Dylan ran his fingers softly down her thigh to her buttocks, not stopping until he reached the crease of her full thick ass. His fingers trickled the few inches down until he felt the base of the plug, lodged firmly where he wanted to be.

Inside her tight, beautiful ass.

Kayla definitely had an ass worthy of fucking. Who was he kidding? It was worthy of worshiping, spanking, licking, kissing. It was second only to her pussy, which to him was worth his weight in gold. Her body was pure pleasure and it never ceased to amaze Dylan how he'd managed to go so long without feeling her beneath him. Looking back now, he knew the only way he could have explained his blindness was sheer madness.

"See, I told you." Her words were a mere whisper now. Gone was the hint of laughter that had echoed in her voice earlier. In its place was need.

"Yes, you did." When he brushed his fingers against

the thick device, Kayla shivered. "How badly do you want me to fuck your sweet ass?"

Kayla wrapped her arm around his waist, digging her nails into his side. "About as badly as you want to."

"I don't think that's possible." Dylan grasped the base of the plug and slowly slid it partially out of the tight recess of her ass before plunging it back in with a twist of his wrist.

Kayla cried out in pleasure as she dug her nails even deeper into him. "Dylan..."

"Yes."

"Don't tease me. Fuck me."

"I wouldn't think of teasing you." Dylan chuckled as he released the plug. He rolled them both over until Kayla was flat on her back and he was looming above her.

There wasn't enough light in the room for him to see her as he would have liked. Dylan refused to fuck her ass for the first time in the dark. He wanted to watch it all. To see her expression as he entered her for the first time. He wanted to watch her face as she came, knowing the look of pleasure radiating from her was all for him.

Dylan pushed himself up and away from Kayla so he could turn on the bedside lamp. The room burst into light, blinding him for a moment, but the brief hint of discomfort was a penalty he gladly paid to view Kayla in all of her glory.

With a smile of sweet seduction, Kayla stretched her arms above her head and winked. "Do you like what you see?"

"Like, no. Love, hell yes."

Grasping the rails of his headboard, Kayla seductively asked, "Now that you have me exactly where you want me, what do you want me to do?"

She was so beautiful, completely open and uninhibited and willing to give herself over to him mind, body and soul. The fact that she trusted him with every part of her body made Dylan feel ten feet tall.

"Don't let go," Dylan ordered before pressing a quick but hard kiss to her upturned lips. "I mean it, Kayla. Your hands stay right where they are at all times unless I instruct you differently. Do you understand?"

"Yes, sir."

Her reply couldn't have been more flippant, but it was either give her the spanking she was asking for or give her the ass fucking she was begging for.

The choice couldn't have been any easier to make.

Bypassing her breasts, Dylan nuzzled his mouth against her stomach, slowly kissing and caressing her as he made his way down her body. The heaven between her legs beckoned to him, but he had a little stop to make first. Pausing at the smooth indent of her belly button, Dylan dipped his tongue into its depth, teasing a giggle from her before moving down to the Mecca of paradise that awaited him below.

Seducing Dylan had seemed like a really good idea at the time. But now, spread lewdly, hands bound to the bed by his wish alone, Kayla was rethinking her grand scheme. It wasn't a good idea, it was a great idea. Except she was no longer the seducer, but the one being seduced.

"What a pretty, pretty pussy. I wonder if it tastes as good as it looks."

"There's only one way—" Her smart-aleck remark was cut short by a gasp of pleasure as Dylan silenced her effectively by spreading her lips and drawing her clit into his mouth.

Kayla whimpered as she pressed her hips up to his waiting mouth. Her fingers tightened against the rails, the metal melding with her skin as she gripped it for dear life. Dylan had many talents, his oral skills being at the top of the list as far as she was concerned.

With him, it wasn't just a stab of the tongue here, a licky-lick there. It was pure poetry in motion. He lapped at her, stroked her with his fingers, teasing her G-spot until she thought the intense pleasure would become too much.

His tongue flickered over her with lightening quick strokes. Zeroing in on her sensitive bud just the way she liked. Suddenly the vow she'd given to keep her hands above her head was difficult to keep. She was torn among her desires. Kayla wanted to pull him closer. She wanted to push him away. She wanted to come hard screaming his name.

"Dylan..." His name came out like a desperate whimper. "Please fuck me."

Instead of replying, he continued his sexual torture

until she broke like a wild mare under him, bucking and whimpering as she came. Her orgasm washed over her like a tidal wave, drowning her in a sensual bath of pleasure.

"Yes...yes..." The words poured not only from her mouth but from her soul. The shattering intensity of her release brought tears to her eyes. It was just that damn good. Kayla was beyond seeing stars and hearing angels sing from above, she was awash in a sensual ecstasy Webster himself couldn't define.

As Kayla trembled in the aftermath of her orgasm, Dylan pulled his mouth away from her tender pussy, but kept his fingers buried deep within her. He no longer plunged his fingers into her depths though. Instead he caressed her quivering flesh, gathering the copious juices that shimmered out of her body. He withdrew his fingers and moved his hand up to her breast, where he caressed her nipple, coating the tingling bud with her own dew.

Dylan moved quickly to take her nipple into his mouth before the cooling air could dry her damp peak. He grazed her crest with his teeth before dipping his fingers back into the warmth of her body.

Instead of treating her other nipple to same sensual torture, Dylan raised his damp fingers to Kayla's mouth, outlining her full lips with her own essence before devouring her mouth with a punishing kiss.

His tongue lapped at hers and Kayla tasted not only Dylan but herself. She moaned into his mouth, drinking up their mingling flavors as if it were the house wine of the day. Kayla was drowning in her own senses. His rough touch, her tangy flavor, the feel of Dylan's hard cock ready against her thigh all combined made for a very dizzying kiss. It was a pleasure smorgasbord and she feasted.

She could have stayed under him all night just drinking in everything he had to give, but Dylan had other plans. Breaking their kiss, Dylan pulled back, leaving them eye to eye.

The desire ablaze in his eyes was nothing compared to the inferno burning within Kayla. There was so much she wanted to say, she hardly knew were to begin, but Dylan being Dylan didn't give her time to compose a thought before he delivered his next command.

"On your knees." Dylan didn't ask. He demanded and God help her she loved it. When Kayla didn't obey fast enough, Dylan delivered a stinging smack to her ass, causing her to freeze. Now she was torn. She wanted to obey him, truly she did, but if this was his idea of a punishment, Kayla was tempted to defy him. For the pleasure of him reprimanding her alone.

"Now, Kayla." His command was met with another smack. Kayla's nipples tightened to pebbled peaks as she rolled over to her knees. "That's a good girl. Now let's see just how ready you are."

The bed dipped as he leaned over and pulled open the nightstand, extracting the lubrication from the drawer. He quickly stripped off his boxers and moved back behind her. The way he was positioned blocked her view, but from the slick sound of flesh sliding against flesh, Kayla had a pretty good idea what he was doing. He was readying himself for her, just as she had done for him.

Her heartbeat increased as she felt him move into position behind her. The thought alone of what they were about to do had her pussy pulsating and her arms quivering. At this rate, she was going to come from anticipation alone before he even took the plug out.

"So greedy to fill this hot little hole, aren't you?" he teased as he grasped the plug and pulled it out of the tight confines of her body at a heartbreakingly slow pace. Even though words of protest rose to her lips, Kayla knew better than to complain about his speed.

Dylan was a sexual sadist when it came to the plug. If she wanted slower, he would go faster. If she wanted to use it for anal play, he would order her to take it out. Everything was at his command, just the way he liked it. Who was she kidding? It was just the way she liked it too.

"So hungry for me to fuck you here?"

His question didn't require an answer. They both knew what and who she craved.

"This will never do." Dylan tsked as he pulled the plug free from her body. "But this on the other hand..." Kayla tensed as she felt the cool slick head of his cock brush against her virgin entrance. "Will do just nicely."

Her rosette was slick with a mixture of her own juices, his saliva and the lube coating the head of his cock. The plug she had worn faithfully hadn't prepared her for the feel of Dylan's cock penetrating her. Slowly he pushed against her anus until the head of his cock disappeared past her resisting ring into her snug depths.

"Fuck..." Dylan murmured, as he slowly pushed into her.

Despite his earlier demeanor, Dylan took his time entering her. Every inch felt like a mile, every second felt like an hour, but gradually he sunk into her until there was nothing more for her to take.

Kayla let out a shaky breath, trying her best to relax. She knew the more she tensed up, the more it would hurt, but to her surprise it wasn't as painful as she thought it would be. There hadn't been more than a brief twinge of pain before her body accepted him. The plug had prepared her for the initial part, and Mother Nature had prepared her for the rest.

"Are you okay, baby?" Dylan's voice was as shaky as her legs and Kayla knew he was doing everything in his power to make sure she wasn't in pain.

"Yes." Although okay wasn't the word. She was better than just okay.

She was wonderful.

The feel of him buried balls deep in her ass treaded on the thin line between pain and pleasure. Her body was tingling from head to toe and she felt fuller than she had ever felt before. He was thicker, longer and so much hotter than she could have ever imagined that he almost seared her alive.

"Are you sure?" Dylan pulled his hips back slowly

before he thrust forward once more. "We can stop if you want."

"The hell we can," Kayla disagreed hungrily. The only way he was putting a halt to this was over her limp and comatose body.

Dylan laughed hoarsely at her reply. "As long as you're sure."

"I'm sure. Don't stop. I'm sure." Kayla whimpered, gripping the bed sheet in one hand as she moved her other hand between her legs to frig her swollen bud.

"As you wish." He moved with a newfound vigor inside her. Every plunge into her narrow depths took on a new life, becoming longer, harder and more powerful. The bed creaked under their weight as his gentle strokes turned into mind-shattering propulsions.

Just when Kayla thought she couldn't handle another thrust, her body proved her wrong, not only taking his strokes but begging for more.

Each pleasure-filled moan from Kayla's lips seemed to spur Dylan further until he was pumping into her at full speed. Out of her mind with pleasure, Kayla moaned with every downward thrust. Her pussy was aching to be filled, her clit was so swollen and tormented by her constant diddling that she throbbed.

"That's right, baby, touch yourself as I fuck your sweet ass."

Her arms could no longer support her weight and his thrusts at the same time. The only thing that kept her knees from betraying her and giving out was Dylan's steel-like grip on her hips. His fingers dug into her flesh as he powered within her. His marks on her pale flesh would be the parting gifts of all parting gifts.

"Fuck me...fuck me..." she screamed at the top of her lungs as her climax caught her in its powerful grip, stealing away all rhyme or reason from her mind.

Dylan's growl of completion echoed her own cry of release. Her trembling legs gave out long before her willpower did. With a very unladylike snort, Kayla released her death hold on the quilt and pulled herself forward a bit so she could lay down flat.

"Hold on, baby. Let me pull out." Kayla winced a bit as Dylan withdrew slowly.

Finally free, she dropped down limply onto the bed. Kayla was completely fucked out.

"I need to take vacations more often." Dylan slumped down beside her, his breath as labored as hers. "Do you want me to start a bath for you?"

"No."

"Shower?"

Was he kidding? Kayla could barely move. She could feel the delicious hand of sleep tugging at her. "Just toss a cover over me and leave me be."

"*Now* you're sleepy?" He chuckled. Dylan moved off the bed as Kayla snuggled deeper into the mattress. When he came back a few minutes later with a damp cloth to clean her, Kayla was halfway to dreamland.

She murmured a sleepy thank you, or at least she

thought she did. The drug-like effect of their loving was too good to pass up for polite pleasantries.

Whether she wanted to admit it or not, Dylan was really on to something when he equated sex to sleep. She had gotten more sleep in the last few weeks than she had in the last thirteen years and it was wonderful. She wasn't getting as much work done, but she sure as hell felt better. Apparently he was exactly what the doctor ordered after all.

Chapter Ten

Reaching across his desk, Dylan waded through all the forms and papers, searching for the buried phone. Today was turning out to be a pretty shitty day. The Anderson brothers were officially a bigger headache than a blessing and he was on the verge of firing Mrs. Howard if she so much as looked at him the wrong way again.

Dylan had put up with her high-minded ways for way too long. Somewhere along the way, she had gone from being his assistant to thinking she was his boss, and that was just not going to fly anymore.

If that wasn't bad enough, Dylan had tried to call Kayla earlier today, but she wasn't in and it was just another thing pissing him off. Not that he expected her to be at his beck and call, but a phone call to tell him she was okay and wasn't in any mortal danger would be great.

She was a bit...accident prone, so worrying about her well-being didn't seem like he was thinking too much outside the box. If only she would stay where he put her, he thought with an evil little grin. If Kayla heard him say that, she'd try to detach his retina.

She was a feisty little thing and she was all his.

They had been spending a lot of time together in the past two months, in and out of bed, and things between the two of them had never been better. They'd even managed to work out a schedule they both could be happy with, where Kayla stayed over at his house three nights out of the week, ensuring that after hours of loving, she would finally get the sleep she needed.

All it took to arrange it was Dylan taking two days off and pampering her like she'd never been pampered before. In truth, Dylan wasn't sure who enjoyed their time together more. There was something very fulfilling about spoiling the woman he cared for.

It wasn't as if they were dating, since dating seemed so high school to him. Not dating per se, but the fact that it had to have a name. This was one of the things that had always been a problem with him in previous relationships, women wanting some sign of commitment. But with Kayla, it had never even come up.

That was one of the reasons his and Kayla's relationship seemed different, more special. Maybe it was because they were friends first and she had already known how much possessive women annoyed him, or maybe it was just she was as much of a free spirit as he.

She was perfect for him, not too demanding, except for in bed, and she accepted their arrangement the way it was. No hinting for a wedding ring. No crying because he never said "I love you". She hadn't even said it yet, which did kind of bother him, but not because he wanted her to say it. It was just strange.

Dialing her number from memory, Dylan listened impatiently as it rang for what seemed like the hundredth time. That girl needed a damn pager or a LoJack, so he could keep track of her.

Just as he was about to hang up, Kayla breathlessly answered the phone. "'Lo."

"Where have you been?" he growled.

Pleasure filled her tone when she recognized his voice. "Hey, sweetie, how's your day going?"

"Long. I've been calling you all morning."

"Sorry, I missed you. I was out."

"Well, I figured that, seeing as to how you didn't answer the phone."

"Wow, you're in a pleasant mood."

"You didn't say anything about going out." Sitting back in his chair, Dylan's mood began to improve by just listening to her voice. "I was worried."

"You don't have to worry," she said softly. "I'm a big girl."

"Yes, I know." Dylan thought this was the perfect moment for her to prove it.

Lowering his hand to his pants, he unbuckled them as he said, "So, what are you wearing?"

"I can't right now," Kayla chuckled. "I'm having company."

Feeling disappointed, Dylan buckled his pants back up and frowned. "A client?"

"No." Excitedly, she said, "I'm meeting with one of my

volunteers today."

"What?" exclaimed Dylan, sitting straight up.

"Yeah, I talked to Missy at Harris's and—"

"Harris's Adult Video?"

"Yes, and she found a few people who'll do it."

Dylan's blood began to boil. He couldn't believe what he was hearing. Of all the hare-brained ideas Kayla had ever had, this was by far the worst.

"Let me get this straight." Speaking very softly, Dylan slowed his breathing down, trying to calm himself. "You went to a *porn* store and had one of the workers ask the clients if they would be interested in allowing you to shove a vibrator up their ass. And you're going to be interviewing them in your apartment. Alone. Today."

"The way you put it makes it sound so seedy," grumbled Kayla.

"What are you thinking?" That was the problem, she wasn't thinking. Someone needed to shake some sense into her before she ended up dead on the side of the road.

"Don't talk to me that way, Dylan." Her voice lowered and Dylan could tell by her tone she was getting upset, but he honestly didn't care. She was putting herself in danger by continuing with this stupid thing. It was one thing for her to tinker with her *toy*, but a completely different thing for her to solicit men to try it out.

Counting to ten, Dylan tried his damnedest to get himself under control. Arguing with Kayla would get him nowhere. "Look, I'm sorry if my tone offends you, but you have to realize how silly this is."

"Silly?"

"I mean this walnut thing is ridiculous. Just another one of your crazy ideas that's never going to pan out."

"Silly. Ridiculous. I don't happen to think so!" she yelled into the phone.

She was the only one. "Kayla..."

"Don't Kayla me. I'll see you when you get home."

"Don't you dare—" His words were cut off as she did exactly as he was warning her not to do. Dylan swore as she slammed the phone back into the receiver. Angrier now then when they first started arguing, Dylan hung up, swearing under his breath the whole time.

What the hell was she thinking?

Fuming, Dylan got up from behind his desk and headed towards the door. Chris entered the office just as Dylan reached it.

"Hey, where are you going?" Chris held up his hand, barring Dylan's exit.

"I've got to go home."

Chris stared at him as if he had lost his mind. One look at him and Dylan knew why. Chris had walked in carrying an arm full of folders they were supposed to be going over. Something Dylan had asked him to do not even a half an hour ago.

Pushing the door closed behind him, Chris walked past Dylan to his desk and dropped the folders on top. Dylan swore under his breath. He knew he wasn't getting out of here without some sort of explanation, but he didn't even know where to start.

"What's up, man? What's going on?" Chris questioned.

"Kayla, she's driving me crazy."

"What, more phone sex?"

That comment caught Dylan totally off guard. He could even feel himself starting to blush. He didn't know Chris knew about that.

Chris burst out laughing at Dylan's expression. "You don't think you're fooling anyone around here, do you? You're taking phone calls in the middle of meetings, shutting your door to make calls, and please, could you open a window in here every now and again? You're office is beginning to smell like my room did when I was a kid."

Dylan grimaced at the visual building his head.

"That bad, huh?" he said, as he sat down on the couch in his office.

Chris nodded and grinned. Grabbing the chair in front of Dylan's desk, he carried it over to the couch and turned it so that the back of the chair was facing Dylan. Straddling it, he crossed his arms on the top. "What's going on with you two, man? I thought things were going great."

Dylan was so fed up, he just blurted out the truth. "They are, normally, but she's got this hare-brained idea to test out her anal wand on..."

"Anal wand?"

"Walnut Wand, whatever, on these guys she met at a porn store."

Chris sat up straight, his eyes as wide as headlights. "Either your sex life is a whole lot kinkier than I thought, or you need to back up and give me a play-by-play."

Sighing, Dylan leaned his head back on the couch and closed his eyes. "She drives me crazy. She's like a big kid. She doesn't sleep, eats in bed, and goes a mile a minute. I don't mean talking fast, I mean she does everything fast."

Looking up, he noticed Chris smiling and frowned deeper. "She's always on the go. I can't remember the last time she shaved her legs and she comes up with the craziest ideas."

"Like the Walnut Wand?"

"Exactly, what sane person thinks up sex toys?"

"One with a vivid imagination, I'd say."

"Don't get me started on her imagination." Raising an eyebrow, he continued, "Do you know she's afraid of clowns? I can't even eat at McDonald's anymore. If I do, I have to take it out of the bag before I bring it home."

Laughing, Chris shook his head. Dylan knew he sounded foolish, even to himself, but as far as he was concerned, they were all valid points, proving Kayla was one dish short of a full load.

"Let me ask you a question, man."

"If it's about the Walnut Wand, don't bother," Dylan seethed.

"No, it isn't." Chris smiled. "If she drives you crazy, why have you been walking around here with a smile etched on your face? Why do you leave here promptly at closing time when you used to work late every day? Why are you calling in sick when you've never done it before? Or here's an even better question, if she drives you mad, why do you care if she has strange men at her house?"

Dylan opened his mouth to reply then promptly shut it. What did Chris mean why? Wasn't it obvious? "It's the fucking principle."

"What principle?"

Frustrated, Dylan stood and began to pace back and forth. "You just don't get it, man."

"Then explain it." The reasonable tone of Chris's voice was beginning to drive him mad.

"I can't stop thinking about her. Even though there are a million things about her that drive me up the wall, there's still something about her." Stopping, he turned back and stared at Chris. "I've got to go."

Standing up, Chris shook his head. "We have work to do today."

"I'll be back in an hour. Two, tops," he said, grabbing his keys off his desk. Walking out the door, he nearly ran into Mrs. Howard, who was on her way into his office. He held up his hand to silence her as he stormed past her.

"Where's he going?" she asked Chris, who strolled out of Dylan's office.

"He's taking a lunch, a long lunch." Walking past her, he missed the smile on her weathered face.

"It's about time," she said under her breath, as she leaned over and opened her desk, extracting the air freshener she had begun to keep in her drawer.

Entering his office, she sniffed, trying to detect any unseemly odors. Walking to his desk, she straightened up his papers before opening the window behind it. Letting in the fresh air, she marched back to the door, sprayed the air freshener and shut it tightly behind her. Young men these days, she thought disapprovingly.

Slamming the phone down as hard as she could into the cradle did little to help ease her anger. Never before had Dylan spoken in such a patronizing way to her. Good thing, because if he had she would have hot-wired his house to hell and back.

The nerve. The balls. The gall. How dare he order her about as if she were a child? He wasn't the boss of her. Right now, she wasn't even sure if she would classify him as her friend.

He was an ass and what he needed was a big Walnut Wand to plug his big know-it-all mouth shut. Dylan hadn't appeared to be against her butt plug when he was shoving it up her ass. Nor had he seemed to be appalled by her imagination at Harris's when she had gone down on him in the booth.

But when it was something she wanted to do, alone, without his permission or without informing her self-appointed Lord and Master, then his starchy, overly conservative, mad-hatter side showed up.

So he thought her idea was mad, did he? Who was he to judge? The man was more uptight than Felix from the Odd Couple. Did he really think he was so easy to live with? For his own sake, she hoped he didn't.

Dylan, in all his glory, was far from perfect. He was anal, controlling, domineering, and too rigid in his thinking for her peace of mind. But did she go around trying to change him, trying to tell him what to do? Hell no. She just accepted him, stinky faults and all. To think, she'd been under the mistaken impression he *might* be happy for her.

Ha. Either she was an idiot or he was. In her mind, there was no real question of right or wrong. She was right and he was dead wrong, or he would be when she got her hands around his neck.

"Asshole," she raged at the top of lungs just as her doorbell rang. Turning on the balls of her feet, Kayla faced her front door like Satan himself was behind it.

Satan being Dylan of course.

Kayla wasn't an idiot though, even as mad as she was. She knew Dylan couldn't possibly be at her door so quickly, but still, she stormed over to it and swung it open as if he were waiting on the other side.

Her venom raged bold and crisp on her face, sending her visitors a step back. "Yes!"

"Uh..." The young man nervously looked from her to the other man standing next to him as if at a loss. "We're looking for a Kayla Martin. Maybe we have the wrong apartment."

Damn it, if she didn't watch out, she was going to allow her anger at Dylan to scare away her volunteers. Taking a deep breath, Kayla counted quietly to herself, trying to bring her temper down a notch. This wasn't their fault. This wasn't her fault. This was the fault of the son of Lucifer, and she would make him pay. Later. Right now, she had to get to work. "I'm sorry for that. Let's try this all over. I'm Kayla and you must be the gentlemen Missy told me about."

"Yes, I'm Scott." The young man who had spoken to her stretched out his hand, an easy grin coming to his face. Kayla quickly took his hand, wanting nothing more than to put the whole bad first impression out of her mind.

"And I'm Reed."

Kayla shook the other man's hand before ushering the two of them in. "I've heard a lot about you both, and I can't say enough how grateful I am that you came over today."

I can do this. I can do this. "Please have a seat while I get the survey and some refreshments."

The two men sat down on her couch as Kayla made her way to the kitchen. She spent the majority of the morning cleaning her house and shopping just for this moment and she wasn't going to allow anything or *anyone to* ruin it now.

When Kayla entered the living room again, she'd managed to get her temper back under control. After setting down the serving tray, which she'd picked up just this morning, she pushed her recliner a bit closer to the men so she could talk.

"Before I pass this out, do either one of you have any questions?"

Reed, apparently the shier of the two, shook his head as he reached for a can of soda. Since the moment she opened the door, he'd been avoiding making eye contact. Kayla wondered if he was going to be able to go through with it. Not that she could *really* blame him.

Even though this was her project, Kayla could understand why someone might not want to shout from the rooftops they liked shoving things up their behinds. Hell, it was still a bit unnerving to her, even though she and Dylan had explored that side of lovemaking.

The last thing she wanted was for him to feel uncomfortable, so she sent him a small smile, hoping it would ease some of his tension.

Scott, on the other hand, didn't seem as if he had any such qualms. From the relaxed, almost sprawled out pose he had on her couch to the cocky sureness on his lips, Scott was definitely a man not ashamed to be there. There was a teasing glint in his eyes that said more to Kayla than any words could have. He was absolutely perfect for the Walnut Wand.

"Missy told us a bit about your project," Scott paused,

a large grin breaking out over his handsome face, "but I'm not quite sure if I understand it completely. Could you explain it to us, in a lot of a detail?"

Scott shot Reed a smirking look as the other man blanched and tried his best to scoot farther back on the couch.

"Are you trying to scare him off?" Kayla narrowed her eyes at Scott. He was purposely trying to freak Reed out. If she wanted someone to do that she could have conducted the interview with Dylan looming over them.

"Not at all. I just don't think he has the balls to do it."

"I don't need his balls, just his ass." The words slipped out before Kayla could help herself, but to her relief Reed grinned. It was the first sign of life she'd seen from him.

Leaning forward, the shy man picked up the sheet. "If you're only looking for an ass, look no further than Scott. He can't help himself."

"Whatever, man." Scott cuffed the guy in the back of the head teasingly. The friendship between the two of them couldn't be denied. Only a real friend would put up with crap like that. "He's just here for the money. Me, on the other hand, I'm here for the science. Anything to help out my fellow man."

"Then I don't have to pay you?"

"It depends on how good it feels." Scott grinned. His infectious smile and joking comment soon had them all laughing. They were going to be perfect after all.

Chapter Eleven

Dylan made it home in record time, only running one red light and two yellow ones in his haste to get there. Waiting impatiently in the elevator, he played scene after scene of what could be going wrong in Kayla's apartment. Strumming his fingers against his pants leg, he watched the elevator numbers light up as he passed each floor.

This walnut crap was going to have to stop. She was being far too reckless. Strange men in her apartment. Sex toys just lying about. What was she thinking? He and Kayla were going to have to come to an agreement damn quick.

Dylan considered himself a reasonable man, but she was pushing him too far. And she had the nerve to hang up on him. Hang up on him!

When the elevator door finally opened, Dylan had worked himself into a fine tizzy. He was worried, he was annoyed and he was pissed off. And not necessarily in that order.

When he got a hold of her, he was going to paddle her ass until it glowed. His angry footsteps ate up the distance as he stormed down the hall to her apartment.

Dylan drew up short when her door opened before he reached it and two men stepped out. They both appeared as if they were in their mid-twenties, tall, muscular and too good-looking for Dylan's peace of mind.

Kayla's ass would wear his handprint for the rest of her days.

Turning around, the taller of the two men addressed the open door. "I'll give you a call later this week, all right?"

Dylan gritted his teeth, holding back his rage. It would be a cold day in hell before he let Kayla take a fucking phone call from either one of these asses.

Stepping menacingly towards the two men, Dylan gave them his best guard-dog look. Kayla, who was standing in the open doorway, hadn't noticed him yet. In fact, she seemed to not have a care in the world. Her tone was light and cheery as if they hadn't been arguing just moments earlier. "Great, I can't wait to hear from you, Scott. You too, Reed. Thank you both so much for stopping by."

She was alive. That was a good start. Fuming, Dylan waited until the boys passed by him and made his presence known by stepping in front of her door. When Kayla saw him, the smile immediately slid from her face. It was replaced with a scowl as she tried in vain to slam the door in his face.

"I don't think so." Moving quickly, Dylan put his hand on the door and pushed it open.

"Get out of here," she raged angrily at him. "I don't

want to talk to you right now."

"Tough." Actually her not talking was perfect for him. Besides, did she really think she was going to keep him out? Mindful of his strength and anger, Dylan moved Kayla out of the way and slammed the door behind him. Hurting her wasn't his intention, making her see reason was. "Don't you ever hang up on me again!"

Instead of backing down, Kayla stepped forward, eyes narrowed in anger. "Who the hell do you think you are?"

"I'm the man you're fucking," he snarled. "And despite what you think, I have every right to get pissed off when you bring strange guys home from the motherfucking porn store."

Dylan stood in front of her, staring down at her upturned face. Fire filled her eyes as she shook with anger. Kayla's face was flushed and her breasts were rising, much like they would if they were in bed making love. There was a thin line between passion and anger, and it was similar in sight as well as in sound.

"You don't own me, Dylan," fumed Kayla, as she walked away from him.

Dylan grabbed her arm and spun her back around. *Was she fucking kidding?* He owned her just as much as she owned him. The difference was, he didn't share. "The hell I don't."

The animal instinct that every man possessed raged up inside of him and sprung out. Kayla walking away was like a deer fleeing from a hungry lion. His instincts automatically demanded he attack.

Pulling her into him, he ground her lips under his. He couldn't get her words out of his head. How could she think that, say that? She was his, damn it. All his.

The fear and anger he felt poured out of him and consumed him as he ate at her mouth. Kayla was unresponsive for the first time ever with him, and it only fueled his need to have her submit even more.

Pulling her in tighter, Dylan was surprised to feel her arms pushing between them. She was fighting him, pushing him away. Surprised at his own reaction, Dylan broke their kiss and loosened his grip on her.

Breaking out of his loose hold, Kayla jerked back from him and stared into his eyes. The fear in her eyes humbled him, jarring him from his rage.

Fuck! He was out of control.

Cursing under his breath, Dylan moved from her and ran his hand through his hair warily. This wasn't what he wanted. This wasn't what he meant to happen. Turning towards her again, he saw that the fear in her eyes had bled out, leaving only the anger from earlier swimming in their dark depths.

"I'm sorry about that." The disgust in his tone seemed to blot out some of the fury in her eyes, and for that Dylan was grateful. "I had no right to touch you in anger."

"No, you didn't," she agreed stubbornly.

"Kayla, you have to see this from my point of view." How could she not understand how he felt about her? The worry tore at his soul that something might happen to her and he'd lose the one good thing in his life. This wasn't about the wand. This was about her.

"No, I don't. You think I don't understand, but you're wrong. You want a no-strings relationship and that's what I've given you. I don't pressure you. I never ask you for anything, but you are always demanding of me."

Kayla turned to walk away, but stopped short. Spinning back around she advanced towards him again. Hurt unlike anything he'd ever seen washed over her face.

"You know what hurts the most, Dylan? Not that you don't trust me. Not that you think I'm flighty, and you do. It's the fact that you have no faith in me."

Dylan was floored. He couldn't believe she thought that. Of course he trusted her and he had all the faith in the world in her.

"Of course I do."

"No, you don't." Her furious voice shook with anger. "You think my idea is stupid and without merit."

Dylan was at a complete loss as to what to say. Of course he thought the Walnut Wand was a bit stupid. What else was new? He thought most of her ideas were a bit out there, but that never stood in their way before.

Kayla and her crazy plans were just as much a part of the many things he loved about her as was the way she smiled. They all made up the whole of her, and he couldn't imagine her not planning and plotting. It was just her being Kayla.

He realized that, really he did, but that didn't mean he had to agree or approve of her having strange men in her home. This whole thing was just blown out of proportion. She wasn't seeing what he was trying to tell her.

Dylan reached out his hand to her, trying to draw her back to him. When Kayla stepped away from him, his irritation rose up again. This was getting out of hand. "Just because I'm not bowled over by your wand doesn't mean..."

"Don't you get it?" Kayla shook her head, her brown eyes darkening in pain. "You don't have to like the wand. You don't even have to get the point behind it. You're just supposed to support me and believe in me. Even if you don't believe in the idea."

"Kayla..." Dylan tried to reach for her, but she stepped out of his way. Believe in her, of course he did. Didn't she know that? A better question was, why didn't she know that? The only answer he could come up with was that he hadn't told her, hadn't shown her he did.

Remorse like he never felt before flooded Dylan's soul. Kayla's eyes filled with tears and he wanted to die. Stepping towards her, Dylan wanted to pull her into him and comfort her. He wanted to wipe away her tears but Kayla shook her head stopping him in his tracks.

"I've always known what everyone else thought about me, but I had really thought you were different. Silly me for thinking that, huh?" Walking past him, she went to the door and opened it. "I want you to leave."

"Kayla..."

"Leave, Dylan." Her voice was hoarse from tears but strong with conviction. "I don't want to talk to you right now and if you value our friendship, you'll leave."

Despite the fact everything inside of him was telling him to stay, work this out, Dylan knew he had to leave. He'd blown it. No matter how much he wanted to protest and tell her he believed in her, he knew she'd never hear what he had to say. Whether he had a right or not to get upset wasn't the point any longer.

If he couldn't give her the space she needed, Kayla would never give him the time of day again. He knew that much about her.

Dylan paused at the door and looked over his shoulder at her again. Tears ran freely down her face, causing his heart to shatter knowing he was the cause of it.

Dylan knew sorry wasn't what she needed to hear. It wasn't even close to what she wanted to hear. The only real problem was he just didn't know what it was she did need to hear.

For two people who always had so much to say to one another, they were surprisingly mum for the first time in their relationship.

His mind flashed back over the millions of conversations they'd had over the last five years and yet the only thing Dylan could to think to say was, "Call me."

Since Kayla had been a little girl, the park was the place she would go whenever she was upset. Now at the age of twenty-eight, the park was the first place she headed after the disastrous meeting with the bank.

Union Bank had been her last hope, and now her dreams had been dashed by another stuffy man in a too-tight suit, who in no uncertain terms told her his bank wasn't in the business of financing porn.

Porn, ha! What would a stiff prig like him know about porn anyway? From the looks of him, he hadn't had an orgasm since Reagan was in office. If there was anyone who needed to use the wand, it was probably him. Besides it wasn't as if she was going to make an instructional video on how to use the Walnut Wand, she just needed financing to make it.

Without a loan, Kayla had no way of mass producing the wand, once the patent came through. As flighty as she might appear, she knew better than to use up all of her savings. The legal end of the deal was costing her enough as it was. She didn't have much money to spare.

Missy had asked around for her and gotten a couple of more guys from her school to agree to try it. She, of course, had to pay them, but they answered her questionnaire and Kayla thought she had finally worked out all the bugs.

Scott, surprisingly, had turned out to be her biggest find. Not only was he heterosexual, proving there was a market out there for straight men, he was also a marketing major. He had offered to work on the Walnut Wand with her as part of his business final. With his help, things were really moving along.

Of course, if she and Dylan were speaking, she wouldn't need Scott's help. Dylan was a financial analyzer after all. Not that she thought he'd be willing to lift a finger to help her. Of course, at this point, Kayla didn't want his help with anything anyway. It just would have been nice to hear his voice.

Several times in the last few weeks, Kayla had reached out to call him, but then she would think of their blow out and hang the phone up.

The way he had talked to her that day was unbelievable and unacceptable. Kayla would have never thought he could act like such an ass.

It was one thing to be jealous, but to act like a complete domineering jerk was taking it too far. Kayla was utterly happy when they were in the bedroom and he turned on his controlling side. But bedroom antics were the only place she was fine with it.

Kayla was too old and too smart to put up with that shit, so why did she miss him so badly?

Just thinking back to that day made her blood boil all over again. Kayla couldn't remember the last time she had been so upset. Anger was a great motivator, especially when channeled the correct way. She had become determined to make the Walnut Wand a big success and when it was finally on the market she would have Dylan to thank.

When he left her apartment, she had been in tears. Kayla had hurt in ways she couldn't imagine, but then she had turned the sorrow into constructive "Fuck You" energy and worked her ass off finishing the Walnut Wand. And now another closed-minded dick was going to stand in her way.

Depressed, Kayla walked to a bench in front of the play area and sat down. She had a killer headache and she was really tired. She was back to not sleeping again, thanks to him.

The really crappy part was when she normally got into this state, where she was depressed or upset about something, Dylan was the first person she would have called.

He had been her friend, her rock, her biggest supporter and then they had made the mistake of becoming lovers and now she had nothing. No friend, no lover, nothing.

Kayla had gone into the relationship with her eyes open. She knew how Dylan was, but still she'd fallen in love with him anyway.

She tried her best to give him all the space he needed. She never tried to pressure him by saying the words because she knew Dylan. The quickest way to make him run would have been by telling him how she felt. Even now, when she didn't think she could dislike him more, she still loved him.

Maybe that's why his lack of faith had really bothered her, because she knew he loved her too. Even though he never said it, he showed it in so many ways.

And today she really needed him. She needed him to hold her and tell her it would be okay. Dylan had to be the most insensitive, stupid, stubborn, bonehead in the entire world, but right now she wished the bonehead were here.

Rubbing her fingers under her tired eyes, Kayla was surprised to feel moisture on them. She was never one to cry, but she guessed even she was allowed to every once in awhile. Although lately it seemed she'd done more crying than not.

An attractive Latina woman walked over to the bench with a little girl about five years old and sat down next to her. Kayla scooted over as the two sat on the bench, trying to give them room. The woman turned and said thank you and then stared for a moment.

Opening her bag, she took out sunscreen and applied it generously to the smiling child before kissing her on the nose. Kayla looked at her, trying to place her face, when the little girl asked her mother if she could go play on the swings.

"Sure, mami," the lady said, smiling. "Just be careful."

The little girl agreed before running off to the slide. The woman turned to Kayla and asked, "You don't recognize me, do you?"

"No, but you look familiar."

"I work at Thompson and Wilson Financing Company. We've talked several times on the phone and I've seen you in the office, but I don't think we've been formally introduced. I'm Eliza Rivera."

"Oh, hi." Nodding towards the little girl, Kayla said, "I

didn't know you had a little girl. She's a beauty."

"Thanks." Smiling, she looked back at her daughter who was playing on the jungle gym. "Jocelyn is a joy."

Watching the kids play, Kayla felt even sadder. Eliza must have noticed the melancholy look on her face, because she reached in her bag and pulled out a miniature bag of warm gummy worms and offered her one.

Taking it, Kayla felt the tears fall freely down her face as she tried to choke down a sticky, fruity bug.

"Want to talk about it?"

"No."

"Does it have anything to do with my gloomy-looking boss?"

"No," she denied. Looking over at Eliza hopefully, Kayla couldn't help but ask, "He's been gloomy?"

With another smile, Eliza nodded. "Never seen such a whipped puppy in my life. Even the dragon lady is being nice to him."

Kayla's mouth turned up in a quick grin at the thought of Dylan mooning over her. She knew it wasn't right, but damn, it felt good.

"I just came from the bank."

"Hell, I'd be crying too."

Kayla flashed her grin again. "I was turned down for a loan for my wand."

"I'm sorry to hear that."

"Yeah, me too, but the worst part is, it was all for

nothing."

"What?"

"The disagreement Dylan and I had, all for nothing."
Looking down at her hand, Kayla shook her head in
misery. "No wand, no Dylan, no real reason for us to not
be talking any more, and I'm sure Dylan is somewhere
laughing his ass off."

"I'm sure that's not the case. He hasn't looked like
he's been laughing in a while."

"It doesn't matter. None of it does." Looking back out
into the distance, Kayla felt worse than ever. Coming here
hadn't helped at all. Sitting next to Eliza just had her
missing Dylan even more. She had to get out of here.
Sighing, Kayla stood up and turned to Eliza. "Thanks for
listening to me whine and for the gummy worm."

Chapter Twelve

Eliza watched Kayla leave and thought back to how sad Dylan had looked lately.

This must be the Professor he and Chris had been talking about the day she had walked in on them. She had talked to Kayla several times on the phone and seen her around the office, and she recognized her almost immediately when she sat down next to her.

Always making it a point to never butt into other people's business, Eliza wasn't sure what she should do. Part of her wanted to run after Kayla and hug her. In fact, the maternal instinct to do so was really hard to ignore, but the other part knew that she should just mind her own business. Never one to sit back and watch people suffer needlessly, Eliza gathered her and Jocelyn's stuff and called to the playing little girl.

"Come on, mami, we have to go."

"But we just got here, Momma." She pouted.

Running her hand down the side of Jocelyn's face, Eliza smiled. God, she loved this child. "I know, mami, but we'll come back. I have to stop by my job for a minute."

"You said you had today off."

"I do. I just have to run by real quick. We won't be long, and we'll go for ice cream afterwards."

With a squeal of delight, Jocelyn grabbed her mother's hand and started pulling her towards the car. Laughing, Eliza shook her head and was once again amazed at the way a kid's mind worked.

The drive to the office took less than five minutes and Jocelyn chatted up a storm in the back seat. Eliza cherished these moments the most, when it was just she and Jocelyn together. When they arrived at the office, Jocelyn grabbed her Dora the Explorer backpack and pulled it out of the car.

Sighing, Eliza looked at her daughter, bemused. The backpack was like life support to Jocelyn. No matter where they went, she had to drag it along after them.

"I don't plan to be here that long,"

"It's for just in case, Momma."

"Okay." smiled Eliza. Just in case had become Jocelyn's new catch phrase. Everything was now "just in case". It was an annoying little phrase Jocelyn was running into the ground.

The two walked into the air-conditioned building and sighed appreciatively when the cool breeze wafted over their skin. Their car didn't have any, so it was a refreshing change to be somewhere that did.

Walking over to her desk, Eliza picked up Jocelyn and set her in the chair. It was a slow day, which was why Chris had let her take it off. If things went right, she would be in and out before anyone noticed Jocelyn sitting there.

"Sit here, mami. Don't touch anything," she said sternly. Chris was a generous boss and all, but Eliza didn't want to chance pissing him off. "I'll be back in a couple of minutes."

"Okay," she replied, opening up her backpack and getting out her coloring book.

Walking down the hall, she headed to Dylan's office. Mrs. Howard was front and center as usual, with sour expression glued in place.

"Good morning, Mrs. Howard. Is Dylan in?"

Her friendliness was met with cold disdain. "I thought you had the day off."

"I do." *Not that it's any of your business.* "But I need to speak with Dylan. It will only take a minute."

"See that it does."

Eliza barely resisted the urge to roll her eyes. That woman was completely, positively unpleasant. Eliza gave a quick knock before she entered. As she expected, Dylan was facing the window, looking as sad as he had all week. Turning when he heard the door open, Dylan looked surprised to see Eliza in his office.

"Eliza, I thought you had today off."

Fine, she was never coming in again on her day off.

Apparently it just threw too many people for a loop.

"I do." Eliza gestured to her outfit of blue jean shorts and tank top. "This is my causal wear."

"Well, what can I help you with?" he asked, gesturing for her to have a seat.

Shaking her head, Eliza walked behind the chair and rested her hands on the back of it. "I ran into your friend Kayla at the park today."

What she said must have shocked him because in the middle of sitting, Dylan stopped and stood right back up.

"Is she okay?" His voice was harsh from worry.

"I don't think so. She was crying."

"Crying?"

"Yes, she said something about not getting a loan for her wand."

"Christ." Dylan closed his eyes and shook his head.

"She seemed to think you'd be happy about it."

Dylan opened his eyes, and Eliza could tell by the pain radiating from them that her last remark had cut him deeply. Apparently Kayla didn't know him as well as she thought she did. "But she also seemed like she really missed you. I think you should call her."

"I will," he quietly remarked. Looking at her, he gave Eliza a small smile. "Thanks for stopping by and telling me, especially on your day off."

Feeling like the bearer of bad news, Eliza tried to hide her remorse behind a radiant smile. "No problem, boss," she joked. "Keep me in mind when Christmas bonuses come up."

Smiling weakly, Dylan nodded before sitting down. Eliza walked quietly out of his office and shut the door behind her. Saying goodbye to Mrs. Howard, she walked downheartedly back to her area. Maybe coming here hadn't been a very good idea after all. Instead of making things better, she only seemed to have made them worse.

Just when she thought she could make her escape, she realized her earlier hope of getting in and out before anyone noticed Jocelyn had been a futile one.

Sitting on her desk was Chris, who was talking to a beaming Jocelyn. Eliza's heart filled with love to see the two people she cared most about laughing and playing. This was the first time she had ever brought Jocelyn to the office and she was surprised by the way Chris seemed to be responding to her.

Chris looked up when she approached her desk and the smile on his face quickly dropped away when he saw her. Eliza was taken aback at his response. He had always been more than friendly towards her. Chris had shown an interest even in taking things further, a step she was more than willing to take and so she was surprised at his cold expression.

"I see you met my daughter."

"Yes," he replied. "I was unaware I had hired a new secretary."

Surprised flashed across her face at his demeanor. "Sorry, Mr. Wilson." She called him by his last name, something she never did. "It won't happen again."

Nodding firmly, he backed away from her desk as she went around to get Jocelyn.

"Time to go, mami." Eliza quickly gathered Jocelyn's things together. Even bent over her desk with her back to him, Eliza could tell Chris was watching her.

He was always watching her. She could feel him. Feel his desire for her, but he never approached her. Eliza had done almost everything she could think of except strip naked and do the hokey-pokey on his desk to get his attention. Although now, seeing the way he was with Jocelyn, she guessed it was a good thing she hadn't done anything so foolish.

Eliza had always had a firm rule when it came to dating and Jocelyn. If they didn't seem to like kids, she didn't even waste her time. No sense spending valuable time on someone she'd never have a future with. She was very sad to find out Chris was one of those men though. Eliza could have imagined spending a lifetime with him.

"Bye, Mr. Chris," Jocelyn said, looking up at the towering man.

To Eliza's surprise, Chris smiled at Jocelyn. It didn't make any sense. Just two seconds ago, it seemed like he was ready to fire Eliza for bringing Jocelyn in.

And if his smile hadn't been shocking enough, he actually rustled his hand though Jocelyn's hair before adding softly, "Bye, kid."

What the hell! Was he trying to confuse her on purpose?

Looking up from Jocelyn's beaming face, Chris eyed

Eliza disappointedly before turning and going into his office. Confused, Eliza watched him firmly close his door. *Talk about mixed signals*, she thought. It didn't seem like he knew what he wanted.

Chapter Thirteen

Dylan sat behind his desk with his head between his hands. He was really hurting right now, but mostly for Kayla. Just thinking that she thought he would be happy her project failed hurt him in ways he couldn't explain. Sure, he hadn't been the most supportive person, but he didn't want her to fail.

Kayla must not think too much of him to say such a thing. Not that he could blame her. He hadn't exactly been shouting "Hey, my lady makes anal toys!" from rooftops. Their last conversation had left him looking bad, but still, he cared for her. He more than cared for her, he loved her. And if this was important to her, then Kayla was right, it damn sure should have been important to him.

Leaning his head forward, he banged it repeatedly on his desk. She deserved better, but damn it, he wasn't noble enough to give her to someone who was better. Like it or lump it, she was stuck with him. Undeserving, untrusting, anal-retentive him, and she damn well better learn to deal with it. Pulling up one more time, he banged his head for all he was worth into the desk.

"Do you really think that's going to help, sir?"

Looking up, Dylan groaned inside at the sight of Mrs. Howard frowning in his doorway. As he rubbed his reddened forehead, he wondered if the pain in his head was worse than the pain in the ass entering his office. As usual, her brows were puckered in disapproval.

"I'm not in the mood, Mrs. Howard," grumbled Dylan.

She made a very unladylike noise in the back of her throat and turned to leave. Dylan was tired of this. If she was so unhappy here, why the hell did she stay?

"How long have you worked here?" His question stopped her in her tracks.

"Three years ,sir."

"And after three years, don't you think we've moved past the Mrs. Howard stage? Really, is there a particular reason why I can't call you by your given name?"

Turning around, Mrs. Howard's normally stern stare was replaced by a cool one. It wasn't any friendlier, but it was a lot more open. "Well, Mr. Thompson, you never asked."

Stunned, Dylan's mouth fell open. "Of course I did."

"No, sir, you didn't. You just assumed that it was okay." Looking down her nose at him, she appeared regal and righteous.

After all these years it boiled down to respect, he thought in amazement. Maybe the Dragon Lady wasn't so fierce after all. Feeling ashamed and slightly stupid, Dylan stood and walked over to her. His face burned with shame as bright as the red mark on his forehead.

As formally as he could, he requested in his most respectful tone. "Mrs. Howard, would it be possible for me to call you by your first name, Lindsey?"

Nodding her head slightly, she replied as formally as he had asked, "Yes, Mr. Thompson, it is."

Dylan smiled, feeling more at ease and put his hands in his pocket. "Feel free to call me Dylan."

"If it's alright with you, sir, I think I'll stick with Mr. Thompson."

"That's fine." He sighed. Dylan wondered what she would do if he insisted that she call him by his first name. The image of her wilting and keeling over popped into his head, forcing him to bite back a chuckle. Every journey begins with one step, he thought, and maybe in three more years he'll get her to call him by his name. Or even better, maybe he could drink his coffee without worrying if she spat in it.

Lindsey walked out of his office as regal as a queen, head held high and pride intact.

It took a heck of woman to move past protocol and be open to change. And if she was willing to do that for him, a man she didn't appear to like too much, then he should be willing to do it for a woman he loved. With Lindsey, it had all boiled down to respect and with Kayla, it all boiled down to faith.

Glancing at the clock on the wall, Dylan hurried over to his desk and pressed the button on his intercom.

"Lindsey," he said, testing the sound of her name out

on his tongue. It felt odd and somewhat not quite right, but he wasn't going back to Mrs. Howard.

After a pause, she replied coolly, "Yes, Mr. Thompson."

"Could you please ring up Mr. Rosenberg at City Financial? I need to talk to him today. It's very important."

"Yes, Mr. Thompson."

Dylan sat down at his desk and hoped Stan was in. If Kayla wanted a little faith, he'd give it to her. He'd be willing to walk through the fires of hell for her, so walking on water didn't seem too hard.

After making two stops before heading home, Dylan stood outside Kayla's door, nervous and anxious. He had his key in his pants' pocket, but he wanted to give her the option of admitting him or not. Not wanting to take anything for granted, he knocked on her door and prayed she let him in.

When Kayla opened the door, he wanted to shout for joy. But one look at her saddened face shot that plan to hell and back.

She looked a mess. Dylan could tell she had been crying. Her brown eyes were bloodshot, almost as red as the nose she kept blowing. She was in baggy sweats and a T- shirt and it looked as if she had been lying down because one side of her hair was flat and slightly raised.

She seemed slightly unsure if she wanted him to come in, but good manners seemed to win out, and she stepped back and admitted him into her apartment.

Shutting the door behind him, Kayla walked into the kitchen and threw her dirty tissue in the trash. She tried to distance herself from him by walking around the kitchen counter to stand, leaving him no other option but to stand on the other side of the counter.

He wanted to be closer to her but if this was the way she wanted it, then he would respect her wishes.

Kayla crossed her arms across her chest. She gave him a level stare and gestured for him to speak all without saying a single word to him.

She wasn't talking to him.

He got that.

Unsure of where to start, Dylan thought about the most important reason for his visit. "I was a dick."

"And…" she stated as if that was obvious.

"And I don't blame you if you hate me forever." Holding up his hand to stop her from saying anything, he continued, "But I'm here to say I was wrong. You were right. I was being a controlling, insensitive jerk and I'm sorry."

"If you think that saying you're sorry is going to—"

"I may be dumb, but I'm not totally clueless." Her lips twitched as if to smile, but she quickly got it under control. The hand gripping his heart eased a little. "I'm only saying sorry to let you know that I am, not to make up for anything."

"Look, Dylan," she sighed, "I've had a long day."

"Yes, I know," he said, tilting his head a little. "Eliza came by today and told me she saw you in the park."

That seemed like the wrong thing to say. Fire flamed in her eyes and she stormed around the counter faster than he would have thought was possible. She rounded on him, brought up her hand and pounded her finger into his chest. Kayla started pushing him backwards from the power of her poking, so much so that Dylan had to grab the counter to steady himself.

"If you came over here to gloat about how you were right and I was wrong," she fumed, "you picked the wrong time, buddy!"

"Whoa!" he said, throwing up his hands to ward her off. She was heated. Kayla's eyes were no longer shining from tears, but shining from anger. "I—"

"I'm tired of rigid, self-righteous bastards dictating to me about what I'm doing. It's not porn, it's not filthy and it's not stupid!"

"I know, sweetie."

Fresh tears clouded her eyes, and Dylan could tell that she was fighting really hard to hold them back by the way she was blinking rapidly and sniffing

"Don't call me sweetie!" she demanded, as the dam broke and the tears cascaded down her face. "I don't need you. I don't need any of you."

Groaning, Dylan pulled her into his embrace and held

hcr while she cried. The heart clenching had returned. Dylan ran his hand down the back of her head soothingly, trying to comfort her. Trying to comfort himself.

"Well, I need you," he said softly. "And I'll always need you. You can try to push me away but it won't work."

He wasn't lying. Dylan needed her more than he'd ever needed anyone in his life. She was his life. The very blood that flowed through his body keeping him alive. Since they'd been apart, he'd felt like a man who was only half alive. Just being here with her, standing next to her breathing the air that surrounded them made him feel whole again. She was his world and the only person who didn't seem to know it was her.

Kayla sobbed brokenheartedly in his arms until there were no more tears left to cry in her body. Pulling away from him, she stood on her tiptoes, reached over the counter and tore off a napkin from the roll.

Since there was no graceful way to blow your nose, she just let it rip. Dylan smiled at her Kayla-like action and followed behind her as she made her way over to the couch.

Sitting down, she drew her legs up onto the cushion and wrapped her arms around her knees. Looking straight ahead, she stared at the wall as if she were lost in thought.

Dylan sat down next to her and watched as she tried to come to grips with her emotions. The silence was uncomfortable, stiff and filled with so many things unsaid and so many things that should have never been said.

Once again, "I'm sorry" just didn't seem like enough.

Finally, when Dylan thought he'd go mad from the stillness, Kayla spoke. "I feel like an idiot."

"Why?"

"For blubbering in front of you like a baby."

"Kayla," he waited until she looked at him before he continued, "you can cry in front of me."

"I don't want to cry anymore." Looking down at her knees, Kayla's sadness radiated off her. Her voice was rough and thick from tears and she looked like she would start round three at any second. "You should have seen the way he was looking at me. As if I was dirty."

"Don't let his shortcomings affect how you feel about it."

"But it wasn't just him, Dylan. It was a day full of men just like him. I've tried everything I could think of." Sounding dejected, she leaned her head against her knees. "Maybe you all were right. Maybe it was the stupidest idea I ever had."

"Don't say that."

"Why wouldn't I think that? You do."

"Kayla, I believe in you."

She snorted in disbelief.

"I do, and I'll prove it." Reaching inside his pants pocket, Dylan pulled out a folded rectangular piece of paper and handed it to her. It was slightly crumbled from being in his pocket but it still served the same purpose. Waiting patiently, Dylan held it out until she grudgingly took it from him.

Looking suspicious, Kayla unfolded it and gasped when she saw what it was. It was a bank draft made out to her for seventy-five thousand dollars. She stared at it for a few seconds as if trying to comprehend what it was.

"Where did you get this money?" she asked, bewildered. "Better yet, why are you giving it to me?"

"Because you need it."

"No, I don't need your money and I don't need your pity." Upset, Kayla threw the check at Dylan. She watched in satisfaction as it bounced into him and fluttered onto the floor. It might have been petty, but it made her feel a tad better.

"I don't pity you," he remarked, bending over and picking up the discarded check. "How can you pity someone who is so full of life that they glow?"

Ignoring him, she asked, "Why? It's not like you think the idea is any good."

Smiling at her with all the love he felt inside of him, he answered with his heart. "It's because I believe in you, Kayla."

Snorting in disbelief, Kayla dropped her legs back on the ground. "Right, now you do."

"No, I always did."

"Where did you get the money from?"

Looking down at the check, he smiled and ran his fingers across it before folding it into her fingers. "Let's just call it a donation from Dylan's Dreaming Fund.

You're the biggest dreamer I know, so I figured you should have it."

As if a light had suddenly gone on in her head, Kayla widened her eyes in shock. The money he had been setting aside for over the last two years, he was now giving to her.

"This is your house-building fund."

"No, it is my future-building fund, and I want you to be a part of it."

"Dylan, I can't take this," she insisted, trying to hand him back the check.

"You can and you will," he said, reaching out and closing her hand around it. "It's an investment, Kayla."

"It's an investment you don't even believe in." Snatching her hand away, Kayla stood up and walked towards the window.

"I believe in you," he softly said from behind her.

"But if it doesn't pan out, you'll lose everything," she stressed, turning back around and facing him. "Your money, your dream house. I can't jeopardize that on a dream."

"I'm not jeopardizing anything. I'm investing in you."

"But how can you invest this money? What if it doesn't sell?"

"It will." His gaze flicked slowly over her face, trying to gather what she was thinking from her expression. Kayla, normally a very easy person to read, was guarding her emotions carefully.

"But what if it doesn't?" she insisted. "How can you just sit there calmly and put your future at risk?"

Walking over to her, Dylan took her hand once again in his. Running his free hand lovingly down her hair, he peered deeply into her eyes. All of the doubts she had were byproducts of his actions and the bank's deeds. Kayla was the most self-assured person he had ever known and to see her this uncertain tugged at his heart. The worse part was knowing he played a small part in it.

"Because you were right about all those things you said to me, every single thing but one." Looking deeply into her eyes, Dylan said, "I might not be the biggest fan of the wand in the world, but I'm *your* biggest fan, and if there's anything, anything at all that I have, it's faith in you."

"Dylan, I can't," she said, once again handing him back the check. "I know your heart is in the right place, but I can't risk it for you."

Looking down at her, Dylan nodded his head. He knew that was going to be her response. He didn't expect anything less from her. "Well, if you won't accept the check, will you accept this?" Reaching into his pocket, Dylan pulled out a small black jewelry box and handed it to her.

Kayla felt her mouth drop comically. Even though she knew she must look like an idiot, she just couldn't pull herself together. Dragging her gaze away from the velvet box, she looked up at Dylan in shock. Her heart beat rapidly in her chest as if she had just run a marathon. This could not be happening, she thought weakly as she stared into his shining eyes.

"This has been the longest two weeks of my life." His voice broke, clouded by tears. "I think I took for granted what seeing you everyday and having you in my life really meant until it was too late. Every morning I would unlock the door and pray to hear you come swishing in, full of laughter and life. And every day when you didn't come, a part of me died a little inside because it was another day without you."

Tears clouded Kayla's eyes again, distorting her vision. She covered her mouth with her hand and felt the tears slide freely from her eyes. With no shame or embarrassment, she wept with joy

Pulling the lid back on the box, Dylan held it out in front of her and got down on one knee. "I love you, Kayla Martin. I want to spend the rest of my life wondering what will happen when I turn on the microwave. I want to explain the X-Files to you in bed every night and replace cabinet doors that are dented from your feet." Smiling, he added as an afterthought, "I would say I want to hold you in my arms as we go to sleep, but since you don't sleep that won't work."

Bursting out laughing, Kayla dropped her hand and smiled through the tears at him.

Dylan grabbed her discarded hand and held it as he proclaimed. "So instead I'll say I want to go to sleep at night knowing that you're puttering around in the other room, inventing something that will baffle and confuse me. I want to make love to you every day. I want to have kids with you that tinker and putter around and who have your smile.

"I want..."

Raising her other hand, she pressed her fingers against his lips to silence him. Love shone through her sparkling eyes. "It's always about you. What about what I want?"

Dylan smiled up at her. "Tell me, what do you want?"

"I want you to put that beautiful ring on my finger, carry me into that bed and make sweet passionate love to me, and I want you to love me for ever and ever."

"Finally, a plan of yours that I can actually get into." Glowing with happiness, Dylan took the ring out of the box and held it in front of her finger. The ring was white gold and the diamond was princess cut, beautiful and simple, just like she would have picked.

"Kayla, will you marry me?"

She nodded with tears pouring from her eyes. "Yes, Dylan, I will." As he slid the ring on her finger, Kayla was not surprised to see the ring, like Dylan, was a perfect fit.

She was overcome with joy. Like so many other little girls, Kayla had always imagined what this day would be like. Although a little off the mark, it was still just as magical as she had always dreamed it would be.

Standing up, Dylan lowered his head and brushed his lips against hers. Kayla smiled through the tears in her eyes as she wrapped her hands around his neck and brought him in closer to deepen in the kiss. His tongue slid between her open soft lips and swept against her waiting tongue.

Pulling back, he withdrew his tongue, pausing to gently kiss her slightly opened mouth. Taking her hand, heavy with his ring, he led her to the bedroom. Standing in front of one another, they began to undress, their clothes seeming to fall away as they hurried to be with one another.

Walking towards him, she ran her hands down his bare chest, scratching her nails lightly across his nipples. He bent over, scooped her up and laid her on her back on the bed. Lying down next to Kayla on his side, he bent down and peered into her eyes.

"Have I mentioned how much I love you?" he asked huskily, running his hand through her soft hair.

Reaching up, she caressed his cheek, rubbing her thumb over his bottom lip. "If I say no, will you say it again?"

"I love you." Lowering his mouth, Dylan brushed her lips with his. "I love you. I love you."

"I love you too," she whispered back.

This is how she had always imagined it would be. He was finally hers and she, like always, was his. All the doubts and all of her fears melted away. Dylan's eyes shone with love, and Kayla knew that hers reflected back the depth of her emotions for him.

Lifting up, Dylan leaned over her, his legs sliding between hers, spreading them as he kissed down her body. Kayla's nipples tightened as he first ran his fingers then his lips over them. Cupping her breasts, Dylan palmed her globes, pushing her nipple up higher and capturing it in his mouth. Closing his teeth around it, he gently tugged as he flicked his tongue back and forth over her erect peak.

He alternated to her other breast, lavishing it with the same erotic torture that he had inflicted on the other, grinding his pelvis against her moist pussy as she arched against him in arousal.

Kayla's fingers pushed into his hair, forcing his mouth harder on her breast as she wrapped her legs around his waist, pulling him in tighter to her. Bowing her back, she cried out in pleasure as Dylan fondled her breasts.

Moving lower on the bed, Dylan eased between her thighs, spread her lips and dove in. He had the best tongue in the world, she thought as he lapped his tongue against her slit. Tightening her hands into his hair, she gyrated her pussy against his mouth and begged for release.

Whimpering, she cried out his name as he took her clit between his lips, tugging on it as he slipped two fingers into her hot channel. The double sensation of being fucked by his fingers and having him suck on her clit sent her pleasure sensors into overdrive, tearing screams of pleasure from her mouth.

Rising up, Dylan wasted no time grabbing his cock and plunging into her. Leaning down, he placed one arm on the bed and the other around her, twisting them until Kayla ended up on top. Sliding back on his length, Kayla eased down slowly on his hard member, trying to allow her body to adjust and accept him that deep inside of her.

Being on top caused his cock to reach areas it normally didn't when he was above her. She could control the movement this way, she thought smugly, as she rode up and down his stiff erection. He felt like hot steel inside her. A hard and unyielding force that thrust deep in her. Squeezing her knees against his hips, Kayla rocked her hips back and forth, milking his cock with the walls of her pussy.

"Fuck." Dylan moaned, grabbing hold of her thighs as she rode him. His fingers dug into her, goading Kayla to go faster.

With his head thrown back and his eyes closed, Dylan bit his lips and groaned as she moved on top of him. Gripping her firmly, he tightened his fingers on her thighs as she sped up her rhythm. Opening his eyes, he glancing down between their bodies and watched as his glistening cock disappeared into her aching mound.

"Ah ah-ah," she teased. "Keep your eyes on me...only me."

"I wish you could see what I see," he said between clenched teeth and from the sound of his tone and the look in his eyes, Kayla did too.

Dylan worked his hand from the outside of her thighs to the mouth of her pussy until his fingers teased her clit, rubbing it in circles as she worked her hips. Sliding up and down his length, Kayla tried hard to find a rhythm but was unable to steady her pulsing body.

Rotating her hips faster, she moaned his name as she came, arching her back, pressing down on him. Grabbing her hips hard, Dylan moved her back and forth, forcing her to ride him harder as he groaned her name and exploded deep inside of her.

Kayla collapsed forward, resting her head on Dylan's sweaty, pounding chest.

Wrapping his arms around her, he held her tight to him.

"Twenty or thirty years of this," she panted. "I think I can get used to it."

Chuckling exhaustedly, Dylan pushed an errant strand of her hair from his mouth and breathlessly said, "Twenty or thirty years of this, I'll be on Viagra and in a wheelchair."

"But imagine what special modifications I can put on your chair."

"Great," he said sarcastically, rolling his eyes at her. "Now I'll be able to operate the microwave and turn on the TV, just by spinning my wheels."

Laughing, Kayla rolled off him and lay back on the sheets, limp and satisfied. Her muscles quivered and her body ached all over. The smell of their loving was strong in the air. The scent alone caused her skin to tingle. Stretching, Kayla relaxed next to him, her mind drifting to a peaceful lull.

"Would it ruin the romantic mood if I said I was

starving?" he asked, turning towards her, laying his hand on his rumbling stomach.

"The only way it way it would be ruined is if you expect me to cook it."

"I want to eat, not throw up."

"See, now you ruined the mood." She laughed.

Getting up, he dragged her kicking and protesting off the bed. Picking up his discarded shirt, she threw it on and followed a naked Dylan to the kitchen.

Hopping up on the counter, Kayla watched as Dylan grabbed lunchmeat from the refrigerator and got the makings for sandwiches. Yanking a piece of turkey out of the package, Kayla bit a piece off and mumbled, "If you're going to cook naked all the time, I do believe you will be in charge of all the meals."

"Sweetie, for the sake of our survival, I think it should be that way anyway."

"Hey!" she said, laughing. "You keep talking that way and I'll update your laptop."

Looking up in horror, Dylan grasped his chest and cried out, "I'm sorry, dear lady, if I've offended you. I'll take it all back. You're the best cook in the world. You're the queen of the kitchen. You're Chef Boyardee."

"And don't you forget it."

Handing her a sandwich, Dylan leaned against the counter across from her and took a bite out of his. He looked devilishly handsome, carefree and happy. Kicking her legs against the cabinets, she stuck out her tongue at his pointed stare and said, "This is my kitchen, I'll kick the counters if I want to."

"Speaking of that," he replied, raising his eyebrow and pointing his sandwich at her.

"Which one of us is moving in with the other?"

"Well, I think you should move in here."

"Why?"

"Well all my stuff is here, and I have more room," she reasoned.

"You only have more room because you hardly have any furniture," he said, gesturing around her semi-bare apartment.

"I have furniture," she disagreed, looking around her apartment. Sure, it was sparse, but it was home. The couch and the recliner were the only real furniture she had in the living room. She ate mainly at her worktable or standing in her kitchen, so she didn't have a use for a kitchen table. Her only working TV was in her bedroom and all of her work was done in her spare room. "And besides, you're not going to let me work on the Walnut Wand in your apartment."

"It'll be our apartment and furthermore, this is the new me, the supportive-husband me. You have my backing one hundred percent."

"Will you try it?" Kayla asked hopefully.

"Okay, you have my backing ninety-five percent."

Laughing, Kayla knew that was probably as good as it was going to get. No need to wish for rain on a cloudless day. If he was willing to accept her and all her peculiar habits, then she should be willing to respect his boundaries. Even if he didn't know what he was missing.

"So, what's it going to be?" she asked, crossing her arms across her chest. "How are we going to solve this?"

"Wanna play for it?" he teased, wagging his eyebrows. Dylan grinned broadly, his eyes twinkling mischievously as he waited for her reply.

"Can I unbutton my shirt?"

"Baby, you're going to need all the advantage you can to get."

"What are we playing?" she asked, sliding off the counter. Unbuttoning her shirt, she flashed him a quick peak of her full breasts before grabbing the cards out of the drawer next to him.

"One hand," he said, holding up one finger.

"Five-card stud," she smirked, remembering their original bet. Dylan laughed down at her as they said in unison, "Jokers wild."

Epilogue

Two weeks later in Dylan's apartment

Picking through the mixed nuts in the can, Chris's stomach rumbled from hunger.

They were waiting for the pizza to be delivered for the poker game so they could chow, but for now he would have to make do with the scraps of food he could scrounge up himself.

Looking around Dylan and Kayla's apartment, Chris could definitely tell their stuff apart. They had just moved into together and although he thought Dylan and Kayla were a great match for each other, he wasn't so sure about their stuff. It hadn't seemed to blend together as well as the lovebirds.

They had different taste and different styles and it was easy to tell what belonged to whom, especially when it was souvenir cups from Burger King, which Chris knew had to be Kayla's, and Lenox dishes from Dillard's.

Although they were complete opposites, Chris thought Dylan and Kayla would make out okay. He had never seen Dylan as happy as he was with Kayla. And after working with him the last couple of months, Chris had decided if they ever broke up again, he would just close the business and take up fishing.

Dylan had been damn near impossible to work with. He had been completely miserable. It was hard to work with someone who was so unhappy. Chris had kept expecting to walk into work and hear Dylan listening to Barry Manilow or some other weepy crap.

Even their poker game was different, he thought, disgruntled. Instead of the usual guys, Kayla had said she had invited two of her friends to play. So much for belching and telling lies. It was one thing to play with Kayla, she was just one of the guys. She was used to them. But to be infiltrated by two more women, that was just asking for trouble.

Not that he thought women couldn't play a good game of poker. Kayla had won three months ago after all. But he was afraid the conversation would end up on periods and hairstyles. And if one person brought up the wedding, he was out of there. It was bad enough he had to be in the damn thing, but to have sit and talk about colors and invitations was more than a guy could handle.

The doorbell ringing brought him out of his daze. Setting the peanut can on the counter next to the cards, he took his wallet out of his back pocket and opened the door.

"It's about ti—"

Eliza stood in the doorway looking extremely hot. Wearing a violet, floral summer dress, she looked sexier than ever. Her beautiful midnight black hair was pulled up, exposing her long, graceful, light brown neck. The way her tresses were styled begged him to pull them loose and run them all over his body.

"Can I come in?" she questioned, looking amused.

Stepping back, he moved out of the way so she could enter the apartment. He wasn't prepared for this. It was bad enough having to be with her at work, knowing that she was just steps away.

"What are you doing here?" he asked ungraciously.

"I was invited to the game."

If she was taken aback by his tone, she didn't show it. For the last few weeks, he'd done everything in his power to avoid spending any time with her. Yet while it was killing him inside, Eliza didn't seem to be fazed.

"Don't you mean you blackmailed an invitation?"

"No." Her smile dropped and her tone changed, expressing her irritation. He wanted emotions. He got them. "Kayla came by the office and personally invited me."

"Look, if you're that hard up for money, maybe you should consider a second job."

"Look, Chris, I may work for you, but on my off time, I'm my own boss."

"Who's with your kid?" he asked rudely.

Chris could tell that was the wrong thing to say by the way she went still and looked at him. "She has a name. Jocelyn is with my mother."

What about her father? Why wasn't he with her or better yet how had he managed to let them go? Either one of them. "Don't you think you should be home with her?"

"I am allowed a night out every once in awhile," she said, putting her hands on her hips. Before Chris could continue his interrogation, Kayla walked up behind them.

"I'm glad you could make it," Kayla said, smiling at Eliza. Kayla briefly hugged her as if they were old friends. When did they get so freaking close?

"Well, at least someone is happy I came," Eliza remarked, staring at Chris.

He was happy all right. Couldn't she tell? This was his happy scowl.

The tension was very noticeable, causing Kayla to glance quickly between them.

"Can I get you a drink?" she asked, breaking the awkward silence. "Now we're just waiting for Scott and then the games can begin."

"I'll do it," offered Chris, looking for any excuse to bail. He needed to get away from Eliza before he said or did something he'd regret, like slipping down the top of her dress and tonguing her erect nipple.

She was driving him crazy. It was hard enough having to work with her every day, but he couldn't even get away from her on his free time. Walking back into the kitchen area, Chris struggled to get himself under control.

Ever since he had found out Eliza had a kid, he had completely backed off.

Immediately placed her in the "couldn't have" column. Chris tried his damnedest to push her away, but Eliza was a hard woman to get rid of. It was almost like she was in heat. He could fucking smell her essence. Hell, he was even tempted to ask her if she dipped her finger in her pussy and dabbed it behind her ears as perfume. She smelled that fucking good.

Opening the refrigerator door, Chris stood in front of it trying to cool off. Just talking to her had him all hot and bothered. She was like a walking, talking wet dream. Sensing her behind him, he turned seconds before she shoved the door, almost closing his hand in there.

"What the fuck!"

"Why are you running from me?" she demanded, closing in on him.

"I don't know what you're talking about."

"Yes, you do. Every since you met Jocelyn you've been treating me like I'm invisible. What? Did she do something rude?"

"No, the ki…" Her eyes darkened, causing him to change what he was about to say. "Jocelyn was fine."

"Then what is it?"

"I don't date women with kids," Chris said bluntly.

"Who asked you to?"

Laughing bitterly, Chris shook his head. "Do you think you're fooling me?"

"So because I don't hide that I find you attractive, it must mean I want to date you."

"Don't you?" he asked arrogantly.

"You're no Denzel, buddy." Her temper flared, sending off sparks in her deep, dark eyes.

"So then what are you doing here?" he taunted.

"Playing poker." She gestured around her as if it was obvious.

"Sure you are." Chris smirked, running his gaze up and down her body lecherously.

"Look, Chris, it's true I find you attractive, but just like you don't date women with kids, I don't date men who don't like kids."

"Its not that I don't like them," he denied.

"Then what is it? Before you met Jocelyn, I thought you and I might..." she said, stepping closer.

"Might what?" His voice dropped, deepening in arousal.

Looking at her, Chris could tell she was just as frustrated as he was. Although he knew staying away from her was for the best, he couldn't deny he was tempted.

But he couldn't chance falling in love with her, because he wouldn't put her or Jocelyn at risk.

"Can we just put all of our cards on the table? You tell me what you want and I'll tell you what I want."

"Fine, you want to know what I want?" Chris bent forward until their faces were mere inches apart. "I want to bend you over that counter and fuck you until your knees buckle and your back bends. I want to eat your sweet pussy until the taste of you never leaves my mouth. I want to have you any way and every way I can think of. But then I want to walk away. No weddings, no playing with the kids, no happily-ever-fucking- after. I want to fuck you and leave you. Can you handle that, Eliza?"

"Well that's not exactly what I want, not that it doesn't sound interesting." Licking her lips, she said seductively, "I want three nights."

"Three nights doing what?"

"Fulfilling three of my deepest fantasies." Running her finger up his tense arm, Eliza reached the top and scratched him lightly with her nails as she brought her hand back down. "Can you handle that?"

"And then..."

"And then after the three nights, if you want to leave, I'll let you. No tears, no begging, no expectations. You can walk out of my life, and I'll let you." Picking up the cards off the counter top, she handed them to him. "I'll play you for your heart and you can play me for my body."

"Eliza, you won't win."

"Do you want to make a bet?"

About the Author

Lena Matthews spends her days dreaming about handsome heroes and her nights with her own personal hero. Married to her college sweetheart, she is the proud mother of an extremely smart toddler, three evil dogs, and a mess of ants that she can't seem to get rid of.

When not writing, she can be found reading, watching movies, lifting up the cushions on the couch to look for batteries for the remote control and plotting different ways to bring Buffy back on the air.

You can contact Lena through her website: www.lenamatthews.com.

Look for these titles

Now Available

Something Borrowed, Something Blue
Joker's Wild: Three Nights

Coming Soon:

Stripped Bare

Anything can happen when Jokers are wild.

2nd book in Jokers Wild series

Joker's Wild: Three Nights
© *2006 Lena Matthews*

Working for your dream man is never a good idea, especially when he's as aloof as Chris Wilson. Eliza's been dreaming of having her boss in her bed for several months now, and when the opportunity comes up for her to spend some of her off time with him at a poker game, she jumps at the chance. Too bad Chris isn't as excited to see her, as she is to see him.

Eliza has gotten under Chris's skin bad. He can't go a day without thinking of his sexy secretary. Chris is determined to get her in his bed, that is until he finds out she has a daughter. He has a firm never date women with children policy that he isn't willing to give into for anyone, until Eliza makes him a little wager. If he wins, Chris gets to have her any way he wants her, and if she wins Chris has to fulfill three of her fantasies.

It's a win-win situation he thinks, but anything can happen when jokers are wild.

This book has been previously published.

This title contains the following, explicit sex and graphic language.

Available now in ebook from Samhain Publishing.

When Elena Richardson mistakes her millionaire landlord for a prospective employee, she'll lose more than just her virginity.

Teaching Elena
© 2006 Maggie Casper

What happens to a virgin who decides she no longer wants to be innocent? While some may go to a trendy bar looking for a one-night stand, others choose less conventional methods.

Elena Richardson is many things, but conventional is not one of them. Hiring a stock boy for her lingerie store seemed like the perfect plan. A hassle free way to get a man past her overbearing brother.

The problems start when Elena mistakes her millionaire landlord for a prospective employee. One taste and she can't turn back.

Available now in ebook from Samhain Publishing.

Fly Away

Discover the Talons Series

5 STEAMY NEW PARANORMAL ROMANCES
TO HOOK YOU IN

Kiss Me Deadly, by Shannon Stacey
King of Prey, by Mandy M. Roth
Firebird, by Jaycee Clark
Caged Desire, by Sydney Somers
Seize the Hunter, by Michelle M. Pillow

AVAILABLE IN EBOOK—COMING SOON IN PRINT!

WWW.SAMHAINPUBLISHING.COM